A WITCH IN TIME

TIME JUMPER
BOOK 1

HEIDE GOODY

IAIN GRANT

1

The alarm rang and Maddie Waites was up and out of bed before she was even awake. Her routine had become so ingrained that some days she could get up, take a piss, wash her face, and be halfway into her clothes before she had her first conscious thought. Those were the good days. When every day was the same grind, it was better to be conscious of as little of it as possible.

Downstairs, Kevin was already up. The dining room at the back of the slim terraced house had been converted into a bedroom, and all the old man had to do to be considered up was shuffle through into the lounge. Lounge, armchair, TV remote, breakfast news.

"Morning," she called as she passed through to the kitchen.

Kevin didn't respond. Sometimes he did. Sometimes he didn't. Selective deafness.

Kitchen, kettle filled, kettle on, check the diary.

Maddie had to put on her glasses to read the diary, which she'd left on the side the night before. Twenty-five and she couldn't read close-up text without glasses or opening her eyes super wide. That was her mum's crappy genes at work.

The thick page-per-day diary was filled with scribbled notes and a carnival of post-it notes, receipts, and other bits of paper. If it wasn't in the diary, it didn't happen. There was too much in a day for anything unplanned to be added.

Today's plan read:

Washing
Mrs H
Work
Chippy
Drying
Gig @ 7

"I'm out tonight, Kevin," she shouted through to her uncle.

There was a buzz from her phone. A message from Gregory which simply read, *Call me ASAP.*

Kevin's laundry basket emptied into the washing machine and put on a timer; cereal out of the cupboard and tipped into a bowl; kettle clicked, tea poured. Kevin preferred it if the teabag wasn't squeezed and it was left to stew, but who had time for that? Bag squeezed, milk in tea and cereal, segmented pill box and breakfast things carried through to the lounge.

It all went on the little camping table at the side of Kevin's armchair. He didn't thank her for them. This wasn't anything to do with selective hearing. For forty years, Aunt Cathy had wordlessly fulfilled the role of the maker of drinks and food. She had barely let Kevin or Maddie set a foot inside the kitchen. Maddie didn't know if it had given Cathy pleasure to take on this role, if it was a compulsion, or if the woman had been indoctrinated by whatever it was they taught schoolgirls in the nineteen sixties. Whichever it was, Cathy Waites had produced the provisions and Kevin Waites had consumed them. He was a product of a lifetime of habits. If Maddie hadn't been there to partially fill the gap, Kevin would have died of thirst, waiting for his wife's ghost to bring him his tea.

"Pants," said Maddie.

Kevin looked down. His dressing gown was open and his blue Y-fronts and pale hairy thighs were on display. He grunted and flung a flap of dressing gown back over to cover his modesty.

The local news segment was on the telly.

"*—An agreement has been reached between investors and local councillors, meaning that Lambert Waris Technical will begin construction of a new engineering facility near the town of Wirkswell,*" said the newsreader.

The town of Wirkswell was in a grassy sheep-farming hinterland that neither Northerners nor Midlanders were sufficiently interested in to culturally claim as their own. There was little local news to be had here, save for tenuous local connections to the national news. An actual local story was a novelty.

"The engineering company is expected to bring up to five hundred jobs to the regional economy."

"Maybe you could get a job there one day," said Kevin.

"I have a job."

"A proper job." His hand hovered over the pill box. "What day is it?"

"Friday," said Maddie.

He popped open Friday's tab to retrieve his selection of blood pressure, prostate, diabetes and blood-thinning tablets.

The clock was ticking. Maddie dressed for work. She set out the gear she planned to wear for the gig tonight. Her bass guitar sat in its case in the corner of the room, untouched for over a week. She'd had no time for practice in a while, but Alice's Demons were just playing the regular numbers at the gig. Flynn would have said if they were changing things up. It was barely a gig anyway. They had, like, a fifteen minute slot among a roster of eight other bands, and the audience would be pretty much composed of just the other bands and their mates. Alice's Demons were in no danger of breaking into the big time with gigs like that.

She called Gregory as she headed out the front door.

"You got my message," he said.

"I haven't got time," she said.

"You don't know what it is. Are you running?"

"What?"

"You sound like you're breathing heavy."

It was short walk up the narrow pavement to Mrs Hawkshaw's house. "I'm just walking."

"You sound out of breath."

"I don't have time for this."

"I need you to meet me."

Maddie rapped on Mrs Hawkshaw's door and the old woman opened it immediately, wrapped in her big coat and a massive, crocheted scarf that threatened to swamp her head, her hamper-sized handbag clutched in her hands.

"See you're ready, Mrs H. Do you just stay there all night, waiting?"

The old woman pointed at the phone by Maddie's ear, nodded in understanding and smiled. They walked together back down to Kevin's place.

"Meet me. Alice's Place," said Gregory. *"What time's your lunch?"*

"I can take lunch wherever. Why do you want to meet me?"

"I have something for you."

"Ominous words from a drug dealer,"

Mrs Hawkshaw gave her a curious look. Maddie attempted a smile but it came out all twitchy. "Lunchtime," she said to Gregory and ended the call. The contents of today's Tupperware box in the top of Mrs Hawkshaw's handbag slopped about gloopily.

"What is it today?" asked Maddie.

"It started the week as chunky vegetable soup, but I've eaten all the vegetables."

"Right. So...?"

"Just soup, I reckon. Enough for two. I brought two spoons."

The unspoken contract between Mrs Hawkshaw and the Waites household was a complex one and, like a quantum physics thingy, not something Maddie wanted to study too deeply in case it suddenly ceased to exist. Mrs Hawkshaw came over every weekday to sit with Kevin, generally potter around the house, and call the ambulance if he decided that day was the day to keel over and die. Mrs H occasionally offered to do a spot of cleaning, but it was a superficial thing: more of a chance to wander round with a duster and aerosol polish. Mrs Hawkshaw didn't do laundry or washing, and wouldn't go near the limescaled and crusty cry for help that was the upstairs bathroom. She brought her own lunch and her own crockery and cutlery. She'd make tea for her and Kevin, but always brought her own cup. And in return…? As best as Maddie could work out, Mrs H saw it as a chance to take advantage of their heating and electricity. The thermostat would always be notched up a couple of degrees when Maddie came home.

"Remember, I'm out tonight," said Maddie as Mrs Hawkshaw settled in the lounge. "I'll bring you both a fish and chip tea for while I'm out."

In the diary, she squeezed '*Greg – weed*' between '*Work*' and '*Chippy*'.

"Make sure it's a nice piece of fish," said Mrs Hawkshaw.

"I will."

"You tell the man I want a nice piece of fish."

Maddie had no idea whether the man would be able to distinguish or care which of his many pieces of fish were the nicest. "I will do that," she said. "Do you want a *nice* piece of fish, Kevin?"

Kevin grunted and waved a hand, as though to indicate

that all pieces of fish were the same to him, which was probably the saner attitude.

"You off to school now?" he said.

"Work, Kevin."

"Same difference." He seemed to properly focus on her. "You look a right Bobby Dazzler today."

Maddie smiled. The endless grind of the days rolled on and, in amongst it, there were moments of niceness, just a kind word here and there from Kevin. Was it enough to make it all worthwhile? She didn't want to think about that question in case the answer was no.

"I might do a spot of cleaning, I might," said Mrs Hawkshaw.

"Go crazy," said Maddie, grabbing her keys from the hook behind the front door as she left.

2

Wirkswell town hall was an imposing building of grey stone probably built as a declaration to the world of Wirkswell's importance as a town of note. But it was a declaration fooling no one, and the windows were draughty and the ceilings on the third floor were damp and mouldy.

Maddie swiped in at reception. The screen told her it was three minutes to nine. She'd cut it finer than that many a time.

The Amenities and Facilities office was on the second floor, so Maddie got the draughty windows but not the mouldy ceilings. The year before, Maddie had put a layer of blu-tak around the frame of the window nearest to her but it seemed to make no difference. In the winter, the blu-tak froze.

Maddie's job was almost entirely an administrative one, ranging from the collation of council documentation on the outsourced leisure centre, to processing the stationery orders from the council park rangers. She didn't know why the park rangers needed so much stationery. Surely they needed litter pickers and wellington boots, not stationery. Maybe they were running a black market stationery shop on the side.

There were three other women in the office. They were all older than Maddie, they all had children, and they generally seemed incapable of engaging in any conversation which didn't swiftly circle round to the topic of their own kids. When it inevitably did, Maddie was only included when one of them told her in a superior tone that she would understand "one day". This was often accompanied by a sad simpering look, as though the only reasons Maddie didn't have children was uncooperative ovaries or her inability to find a suitable baby-daddy.

Telling them she was a lesbian had kept them at bay for a time, but then they had started looking at her with chirpy conspiratorial glances, like she was their special 'lesbian' colleague; another box ticked on their bingo sheet of life. And Maddie wasn't even sure she *was* a lesbian. There were marks in both columns of her boys v girls tally sheet, and having Scarlet Chambers for a girlfriend in year eleven had been more of a social experiment than a relationship. An excuse to go to the Nottingham Pride weekend as much as anything.

As far as the office went, Maddie was happy to be left alone. Computer logged on, earphones in, a playlist of rock music long enough to last the day, occasional interruptions when the phone rang.

"Amenities and Facilities," she said.

"I want to know what this is," came a strident woman's voice.

"What what is?"

"I'm waving one of these yellow plastic things. Someone has stuck one on my windscreen."

"You've come through to Amenities and Facilities. Have you been given a Parking Charge Notice?" said Maddie.

"I have and I want to know why," snapped the woman.

"There is a phone number on the Parking Charge Notice. You can phone that and either pay the charge or challenge it."

"I don't want to challenge it."

"You want to pay it?"

"I'm not challenging it. I'm rejecting it."

"Is that not the same thing?"

"Challenging it implies that I accept it as valid in the first place. I don't."

"You can probably say that when you opt to challenge it on the automated phone number."

"I don't want to automate anything. I know how these things work. I want to speak to a human. I called the council. Have they put me through to the wrong number?"

Sadly, the answer to that question was "No". Amenities and Facilities had notional responsibility for the town's pay and display parking systems, even though they were actually outsourced to a parking company who had their own workforce of civil enforcement officers. Maddie logged into the system.

"Where were you parked?" she asked.

"Were? I still am. I parked on Market Street. I only came in to buy some fireworks."

Maddie clicked on a line in the database. "Ah – I think I see you. Yes. Skoda CitiGo. Registered to Acacia Crescent. You— Fireworks? Bit early in the year for fireworks. It's not Diwali, is it?"

"Is that pertinent?"

"Not to this. Can I take your name, please?"

"It's Bohart. Astrid Bohart."

The name seemed oddly familiar, but Maddie couldn't place it. She almost immediately decided it probably just sounded ever so slightly like Amelia Earhart, who was a famous explorer or something, wasn't she?

"Yes. I can see what's happened," said Maddie. "You used the app to buy parking for zone one-seven-two-six but you parked in zone one-seven-three-nine."

"I am parked opposite the sign. I can see the zone number."

Maddie nodded. "Mmm. Seven-two-six runs from Market Street onto Baslow Road. Seven-three-nine runs from the other side of Market Street into Coomb Street. You can probably see the other sign."

There was a rasping wind on the line.

"So you've fined me because your signs aren't clear enough?" demanded the Bohart woman.

"Technically not a fine," said Maddie. "It's a charge. Like, for a service."

"Oh, a service, is it? Well, I want you to uncharge me now. It's a perfectly understandable mistake, but you can see I paid in good faith."

"I would recommend ringing the automated line and opting to challenge the charge. You can tell them you made a mistake and—"

"It wasn't me *who made the mistake,"* Bohart growled. *"You and your signage are at fault. I have been very understanding up until this point, despite your threats."*

"Threats?"

"This fine—"

"Charge. No one has threatened you, Ms Bohart."

"This sheet says that I have fourteen days to pay. It demands money and says it will be escalated if I don't pay. That's a threat. Textbook definition of a threat. You threaten me and accuse me of making mistakes. Now, since you decided to take this course of action— What's your name?"

"My name is, is not relevant," said Maddie.

"It is if you're the one who is continuing to threaten me."

"Removing charges is not my decision to make."

"Then whose decision is it?"

The haughty tone, like the name, struck Maddie as familiar but there was no placing it.

"Well, it's the system. It's automated."

"Oh, really? Machines have taken over already? Someone made the policy or the decision, did they not?"

"Probably a computer programmer somewhere or...?" suggested Maddie.

"Your name. I will need it for when I escalate this further."

"Again, if you—" Then her brain and mouth made a decision without consulting her first. "Oh, oh, I'm losing you. I think one of us is driving through a tunnel—" She put the phone down.

She looked at the phone for a long moment. "Hmmm. Probably shouldn't have done that." She looked round at the office. No one seemed to have noticed.

"I'm going for lunch," she said to no one and grabbed her coat.

3

Wirkswell Museum occupied the building just round the corner from the town hall. Where the two older buildings abutted the newer shopping centre there was a dingy alley left in the gap behind and a tiny courtyard which was variously full of fallen leaves, discarded cider empties, the smell of piss, and occasionally teenagers meeting up for a crafty smoke.

Maddie and Gregory had been those teenagers at one point, then something had happened and now they were twenty-somethings meeting up for a crafty smoke.

They had always called it Alice's Place because someone had once told them this was the very spot where the locals had burned the supposed witch, Alice Hickenhorn. Or had attempted to, before flaming demons turned up to spirit the witch away to hell. That's what the local legend said. There was a display about it in the museum, and it had given the band Alice's Demons its name.

Maddie put her coat collar up. The wind whistling through the alley was chill but at least the cold kept the smell down. Gregory lit a spliff and offered it to her.

"Morning I've had..." she said. She looked at her phone. "Not got long. Haven't eaten yet. Need to get a Gregg's pasty before I go back to the office."

"Need to get your strength up for tonight," he said.

Gregory had been an underdeveloped teenager when they'd first been friends, then just shot up. Shot up, shot off, got himself a degree and a doctorate, before coming back to Wirkswell to make a living growing weed on the abandoned allotments next to Burnley Manor. Gregory had flyaway hair and a permanently unshaven look going on. Sometimes he looked like a wild and rugged hero. Other times he looked like an unwashed drug dealer. Maddie suspected that, as the years went on, there'd be more 'unwashed' days than 'hero' days.

"I need you to do me a favour," he said.

"I said I'd hand out the flyers and I have," she said, which was a lie.

Flynn (lead guitar and vocals) had said Alice's Demons needed a bigger audience for the gig at the Old Schoolhouse, and Gregory (drums) got a mate to print up a bunch of flyers. Maddie's share were still on her bedside cabinet. If she hadn't got time for bass practise, she certainly didn't have time for handing out leaflets.

"A different favour." He reached into his parka coat pocket and took out a clingfilm-wrapped block.

"Fuck," said Maddie. "You want me to hold for you?"

"My mum is getting suspicious."

"Store it up at the allotments."

"I can't. Foxes got into the last lot and ate it."

"Then put it in a metal box, man."

"I did. Foxes are clever. And looking for their next high. I mean they were seriously off their tits."

"Christ!" Maddie snatched it off him and gave him back the spliff. "I've got to go back into work, you know."

"You've barely had a puff."

"You finish it."

"Smoking in the daytime gives me the shits," he said, taking a drag nonetheless.

"Hardly an advert for your product."

"Keeps your regular. That's what I say."

She made to go but, despite the fact that her tummy was rumbling at the thought of a Gregg's sausage roll, she turned back. "You know, when a friend says they have something to give you, you tend to assume it's something other than a kilo of weed."

"That's like five hundred grams, max," said Gregory. Seeing that didn't cut through her annoyance he fished around in his pocket. "But I do have something for you. Stick out your arm."

"Heroin now, is it?" she said but held up her arm anyway.

He reached out and tied something stringy around her wrist. She pulled back to inspect the thin woven strap.

"A friendship bracelet?" she scoffed. "You are a grown man, you know that, right?"

"It's got your name on it."

She looked. There were three cuboid letters strung on the woven wool. "It says 'MAD'."

"My sister didn't have two 'D's in her box of things."

"Poking around in your teenage sister's box of things?" She sighed and considered it. "This is the lamest present I've been given since ... whenever. And it's also the sweetest present I've been given since whenever. Which is a whole other kind of lame." She stepped back.

"See you at the gig," said Gregory.

Maddie nodded and ten minutes later was back in the office, hot sausage roll in one pocket, pack of Gregory's weed in the other.

4

Maddie picked up two portions of fish and chips on the way home. She did not ask the man for a 'nice' piece of fish for Mrs Hawkshaw because Maddie was not an insane old woman who thought fish and chip men had grades of fish niceness. The hot fat, vinegary smell was delicious, but she didn't get a portion for herself. The price of fish and the crappy combined incomes of her job and Kevin's state pension was not a formula which stretched to three portions of fish and chips.

In the kitchen at home, she shoved a couple of stolen hot chips from Kevin's portion in her mouth and, the roof of her mouth burning, presented the food to the old folks, still in the papers but on plates.

"Oh—!" she said, switching them round and making sure she gave Mrs Hawkshaw a specific plate. "That's the nice one."

Mrs H seemed happy about that.

The house was filled with the scent of furniture polish, but Maddie couldn't see anything that had actually been touched by a dust cloth. She washed up the cups and plates in the sink, took Kevin's cold damp clothes out of the washing machine, and put them over the dryer for the night.

"I'll be back by ten," she called down as she made to her bedroom. "Eleven latest."

She could tell Mrs Hawkshaw had been in her bedroom. There was the smell of furniture polish in the air and, more tellingly, Mrs Hawkshaw had ruined Maddie's clothes. She grabbed the jeans and the T-shirt and stepped out onto the landing.

"What did you do to my jeans, Mrs H?" she shouted downstairs.

"I mended them!"

Maddie balled the clothes in her fists. "I can see that! I mean, what did you—? I mean, why!?"

Ripped jeans and ripped T-shirt were hardly the cutting edge of fashion, but if one was going to be a rock bass guitarist then at least they struck the right note. Ripped jeans and ripped T-shirt that had been repaired with what Maddie guessed was sky blue cotton thread did not give off any sort of rock vibe, particularly since the jeans were a pair of cheap 'comfy fit' ones from the clothes store bargain bin. It was only the rips that had given them any credibility.

"I'll only charge you for the thread," Mrs Hawkshaw called up.

"Oh, right!" Maddie spat.

She threw the T-shirt aside. She'd got an old Nirvana T-shirt somewhere. But the jeans… She ran downstairs, jeans in hand and got scissors out of the kitchen drawer. Her fight with the repair stitching was in vain: Mrs H was a powerfully good sewer and the repairs were like gnarly scar tissue.

"Fine!" she declared and prepared to make some fresh rips. It turned out that denim was also generally resistant to the blade. It took considerable effort, during which she narrowly avoided slicing open her own hand just to get a small cut. She worked on it savagely, dropping the scissors to dig her fingers in and pull it open from both sides. When the denim gave, it really gave, and the leg completely tore apart, from knee to ankle.

"Cunt!" she screeched.

"Language, Timothy!" called Kevin from the language.

"Oh, now he fucking speaks," she seethed.

"Everything okay, dear?" asked Mrs Hawkshaw.

Everything was not okay. Non-ripped jeans were uncool. Ripped jeans were cool. Jeans ripped so there was no fucking lower leg left were deeply uncool. In the bell curve of jean rippedness, she'd gone too far and there was no way back.

She ran back upstairs, knowing now that every moment she wasted was a moment she was going to be late. She ransacked her very limited wardrobe. Did she have another pair of clean jeans? No. Could she wear her work trousers? No. Did she have a pair of black leggings? Yes, but they were tight in all the wrong places and not something she wanted to wear while on stage in front of a judgy beer-drinking audience. If she had a skirt to go over the leggings…

She didn't have a skirt. There was a woollen tartan blanket on the end of her bed. With a decent safety pin, it could work as a wraparound kilt. Kilts were rock and roll, sure. The blanket had been from Maddie's younger days in the Brownies, and Aunt Cathy had stitched all her little Brownie badges and swimming badges to it.

"Wear it inside out," she told herself and set to getting changed.

Definitely late now, she hurried out, bass guitar over her shoulder, in an impromptu outfit of T-shirt, leggings and kilt (not a blanket).

The Old Schoolhouse was a bar and venue on the north side of town and exactly twenty minutes' walk from her house. Maddie knew this because the Old Schoolhouse was her old schoolhouse, the last remaining building of Wirkswell Secondary High before the place moved to a nice shiny campus on the site of the old school playing fields. A twenty minute walk every day for teenage Maddie turned out to be a sweaty thirty minute walk for her older incarnation. Maddie was inclined to blame the chafing of her leggings.

There was already music coming from the Victorian stone building. A guy with a neckbeard was manning the door with a money box and a clipboard.

"Six quid in. What band are you here to see?"

"I'm in a band," she said, angling her bass round.

"Yeah, right," he said.

"You think I carry this for fun?"

"Poser girl more like." He pointed at her T-shirt. "Bet you don't even know who Nirvana are."

"What?"

"Who was the bassist in Nirvana?" he said.

"What?"

"The bassist."

She didn't have time for this. "What the—? I don't need to tell you who the bassist in Nirvana is."

"Okay. The drummer. The drum-mer! Who is it?"

Maddie wasn't sure how the very simple act of getting into her own gig had turned into a pop quiz. The music inside had stopped. A change in bands. It had better not be them up next.

"Look, I'm going to be late," she said.

"The lead singer, then. Come on. That's a gift. If you can't tell me the lead singer then you need to go home and change."

Of course she knew but she wasn't going to give neckbeard the satisfaction of playing his stupid power games.

"Piss off!" she said and pushed past. As he stood from his little stool, she shouted back, "Follow me and see what happens, fuck fingers!"

She stepped into a hall of silent people, faces turned back from the dancefloor and stage, all looking at her in the blue and pink lighting venue light. There was a small cough.

The singer on stage shuffled uncomfortably, hand on the mic.

"—anyway, the funeral's a week on Tuesday and I know Skid's parents – Mr and Mrs, er, Skid – would appreciate people coming along to pay their respects."

The Old Schoolhouse audience were divided roughly

equally between those who were nodding sombrely, those who felt applause was the appropriate response, and those who were glaring daggers at Maddie.

She pulled a deliberately embarrassed face. "Sorry. Coming through. Big love for Skid," she said, moving through the crowd to the side rooms which served as the green room. A couple of bands occupied the space which Maddie guessed had once been a school classroom.

Flynn slouched against a wall in a corner, surrounded by cases and bags. He had a look of cold fury on his proud, handsome face. Cold fury was kind of his stage persona but in this instant, Maddie suspected the fury was real.

"I'm here," she declared.

Flynn looked at her like her appearance was neither here nor there to him. She looked round.

"Where's Gregory?"

"In the toilet," said Flynn. He gestured down at her kilt. "Are you wearing a dog blanket?"

"It's a kilt."

"It's a what?"

"It's a kilt."

"We're due on in ten. This is no way for a professional band member to behave."

"Are we being paid?"

"What the fuck's that got to do with anything?" he snapped.

Maddie decided to say nothing.

"No one has ticked to say they're coming to see us," said Flynn. "No one. And I was just saying to Gregorius that if you're late again then you're out of the band."

"You can't kick me out of the band."

"I fucking can."

"I'm like a third of the band. You can't kick out a whole third. It's a divorce if anything."

"Divorce is between two."

"Trivorce. I don't know. You can't kick me out. Kick yourself out."

"Don't think I won't."

The nearest door opened and Gregory came in. His face was ashen pale and covered with a sweaty sheen.

"Oh, God. You look terrible," said Maddie.

"No. I'm good. Just had a bit of a ... cleanse." He brushed his still wet hands on his T-shirt and frowned at her. "Are you wearing a blanket?"

"It's a kilt," she said.

"I said it was a dog blanket," said Flynn.

"I don't have a dog. It's mine, okay?"

Flynn raised an eyebrow at her. She caught the look.

"Don't you dare. The day I've had..."

"The day *you've* had?"

"Alice's Demons!" shouted the manager from the door.

"Fuck, that's us," said Flynn and waved at the manager before following him out, guitar in hand. Maddie dumped her coat and opened her guitar case – and was struck with an overpowering waft of furniture polish. Her black Squier bass gleamed like the Queen's dining table.

"Christ, Mrs H," she said, picking it up. Its slippery surface almost flew right out of her hand again.

Strap on and gripping it tight, Maddie shuffled through the other waiting bands and tried not to pay attention to the fact that they all looked at least ten years younger than her.

"Cheer up," said Gregory as he saw her catch up. "We're meant to be having fun."

"I don't know if I'm having fun," she said, knowing for a fact she wasn't.

"Ah, come on. Here we are, playing a gig in our old school. It's funny. Like it's fate."

It was bloody crap fate if fate it was, and the crapness of it was the only funny thing about it.

He jerked his thumb back at the green room. "You remember whose classroom that was?"

Maddie looked back and tried to orientate herself over seven years of memory and then it hit her. "Mrs Bohart! Astrid Bohart!"

"Was that her first name?" Gregory smirked.

Astrid Bohart. Maddie knew she recognised the name, and the voice.

"Heard she got fired a year or so after we left," said Gregory.

"For what?"

"Smoking a joint in her classroom."

"Piss off."

"It's true. Damo Papplewick told me."

"Oh, like he's the font of all knowledge—"

A sudden, stomach-flipping thought hit her, prompted by the mention of a joint. Gregory's weed was still in the green room in her coat pocket. Just sitting there, where anyone could steal it.

"You okay?" he said.

"Of course," she said automatically. He looked less well. A tremble passed across his white face. "You?"

He nodded grimly. "Might do some of the songs double tempo. You know..."

"Right," she said and stepped on stage and over to her point to plug in her guitar.

5

The set did not go well. No, that was an understatement. The set of Alice's Demons was such a monumental showcase of rock music awfulness that it was quite possible people would be talking it about for years to come. The awfulness was undeniable. The only questions were which aspects were most awful and what order they had occurred in.

Maddie's bass was out of tune. A week of disuse and the administration of half a can of Mr Sheen by Mrs H had put it so far out of tune that it couldn't be fixed in the thirty second warm up before their first number. Tuning it was doubly hard when Maddie struggled to maintain a grip on its near frictionless surface.

Several of the crowd had recognised her from her interruption of the last band's touching speech for their departed friend and the booing began before they'd even started.

And then Gregory had started up the drumming for the first number, a cover of Devil Preacher's *Lord of the Wilderness*. He hadn't been joking. He'd launched into it at high speed and, even though Flynn threw him a wild questioning glare, there wasn't much he could do about it but join in at the same speed.

Maddie came in with the bass line and her rusty fingers just about kept up, but there were too many bum notes, only half of them the fault of her instrument. Gabble singing at high speed, Flynn did a fair job of holding it together. Maybe he missed out a chunk of the chord changes, but things were flying by so fast that it's likely no one noticed.

Maybe halfway through, Maddie concluded she couldn't succeed here with technical prowess, deciding gusto and showmanship would be the only way to win the day. Musicality would give way to attitude. She thrashed her bass, added some heavy metal head shaking, and after the middle eight decided to throw herself bodily into the final chorus. This was the last mistake of their set and indeed ended it. Maddie jumped forward, swung herself round and, unable to maintain her grip on the polished bass, launched the instrument, headstock first, straight into Flynn's face.

Maddie felt a woodeny *chock* sound vibrate through her bass as it came up into his eyebrow and flung his head back. There was some arm waving and staggering, then he went down, hard, into Gregory's drum kit. One guitarist and two guitars down, the drums demolished by the singer, Alice's Demons' gig came to an abrupt halt.

The complete silence which followed was eventually

broken by someone in the audience throwing an ecstatic devil salute and yelling, "Fuck, yeah!"

A member of staff made her way across the stage to see if Flynn was seriously hurt, but he was already flailing to get up, knocking aside the cymbal stand with a *tshing!* that was far too light a sound for the situation.

"Off! Get off now!" a bloke who might have been the owner hissed at them.

"But we're not finished," said Flynn, although the blood seeping down his face suggested he was wrong on that score.

"And any damages will have to be paid for."

Gregory stood and produced a high-pitched bum squeak. "I need to go," he said in a quavering voice and hurried from the back of the stage.

Maddie went to help Flynn from the stage but he violently shook her off. She had nothing to do but trudge from the stage, slippery bass in hand. Down the steps into the green room, to see her coat laid out on some chairs and definitely in a different position to one she had left it in. She rushed over and felt for the bulge in her pocket. She felt, she re-felt. She searched her side pocket. It was empty. She searched the other just in case she had her pockets mixed up, but there was nothing there except a screwed up paper bag which had once contained a sausage roll.

"No, no, no," she mouthed to herself.

She looked under chairs, in bags, behind cases. She looked at the other bands gathered in the room, but what could she say? "Has one of you stolen my mate's block of cannabis?"

"No."

Elsewhere in the green room, there was a shout of "Holy fuck!" followed by a heavy bass drum hit.

Sick now, feeling tears come to her eyes, Maddie propelled herself up, coat in hand, and did they only thing she could. She went to find Gregory to tell him. The gents toilets in the Old Schoolhouse were the old boys school toilets. Didn't make sense for them to be anything else.

The room appeared empty. No one at the urinals. The toilets had had a makeover since her school days – either that or the schoolboys had been treated to decent tiled flooring and natural wood cubicles denied to the girls. One of the stall doors was closed.

"Gregory," she called. "Gregory, it's me."

She went over to the stall door. The tiles were tacky wet under her feet. She decided not to think about that.

"Gregory?"

She knocked on the door. It swung in. The cubicle was empty.

"Fuck."

She took out her phone to message him, then the door to the toilets opened. Maddie automatically stepped inside the cubicle and closed the door.

"Fucking awesome," a man said. "Best thing I've seen here ever."

"Maybe being shit is a part of their act," said another.

"That's giving them too much credit."

There was the sound of urinating.

"And the female," said the first, irritated.

"You never give a bass to a female," said the second. "It's a man's instrument. If you're gonna have a female in the band, she's got to be able to move about, jiggle."

His companion grunted. "Nothing there worth jiggling. What was she wearing? Like a grandma's lap blanket?"

Maddie wanted to shout out that it was a kilt. More than that she wanted to go out there and rub the unreconstructed incel arseholes' faces in the urinal and tell them that if they were going to diss her, then they should at least diss her for her musicality, not her lack of 'jiggle'. But mostly she just wished today had never ever happened.

The trickled of urination stopped, both streams at once. Huh, synchronised weeing. Maddie waited for them to move, waiting for the sounds of handwashing (unlikely) or the sound of the door. There was no sound.

She looked up. The quality of the light had changed, become dimmer and colder. She waited a full minute. There were no sounds from outside. Okay, this was getting creepy. She pictured them, outside the cubicle, tiptoeing round, shushing each other, suppressing laughs, knowing somehow that there was a woman, a 'female', in their toilet.

"Just piss off," she mouthed to herself.

No. The silence continued and the explanations for two men creeping around with a lone female shut in a cubicle were few and horrible. This needed to end quickly or end badly.

Maddie grabbed the door handled and leapt out with her loudest, deepest, maddest animal roar, either to scare off the evil twats or call for help.

Her roar died. The toilets were empty.

The strip lights overhead were off. The light in the room came from the window, cold bluish daylight.

"What the actual...?" she whispered.

She made for the door. The floor beneath her feet was neither wet nor tacky. This barely registered. It was sodding daylight outside.

The place was quiet, and when she got to the bar she found it empty. It was entirely empty. No people, no lights, no ... nothing.

"Have we had the bloody rapture and no one told me?" she asked the empty space.

This was weird. She went back to the green room. It was equally empty. No bands, no cases. Her black Squier and its case were also gone. She'd have sworn about that, but the panic rising inside her was over-riding concerns for her missing instrument.

She went to the exit. The big old double doors were locked. Even when she unbolted them they were still locked with a key. Trying to quell a rising panic she ran round and barged her way through a fire exit onto stone steps at the side of the old building. The cold air of day was a balm on her face. She breathed it in deeply and looked to the town.

Something about the light and the temperature told her that it was morning, early morning maybe. This was crazy.

She walked. She had to walk.

"Explanations," she said to herself. "You fell asleep standing up and just ... just... Yeah, did that." She shook her head. "A psychotic episode." That idea was oddly more appealing than the sleeping one. "Gregory's weed's tainted. This is all a fucking trip!" she yelled to the sky.

"Mornin'," said a postie, walking past along the pavement.

She twirled as she let him pass. "Er, morning."

She was walking down the hill to her home, pulled by more than gravity. If she'd somehow slept or tripped her way through the night, what had Mrs Hawkshaw done? She couldn't rely on either the old woman or Uncle Kevin to phone her. They both owned phones but had that old person habit of not looking at them or even turning them on unless they were intending to phone someone.

She looked at her own phone as she turned into her own road. There was an intermittent 'no service' message flickering at the top of the screen next to the time and date. The date was wrong. It still said Friday. If this was day, the next day, then this was Saturday. But no, her phone was telling her it was the morning of the day before.

She tutted at the crapness of technology and then saw the woman coming out of her own house. Maddie didn't initially recognise her. She had hair like Maddie's and a similar coat, but she was older in the face, miserable looking. Tired, saggy even. She had a poor, slouching posture as though she couldn't be bothered to make an effort with life. And then, sickeningly, it struck her. That was *her* hair; that was *her* coat; that was *her* own miserable, sagging, slouching self.

Maddie was looking at herself!

The woman turned away and walked along the road towards the town centre. *That* was Maddie, going to work on a Friday morning, the morning of the day previously.

Maddie gasped. "I'm a fucking time traveller!"

6

Maddie watched herself go down the road and away from the house before going over to her own home. She did it automatically and, if questioned (by the time police or whatever), would have said something along the lines that she needed to go inside, to see Uncle Kevin and Mrs Hawkshaw and anchor herself to the real possibility she had leapt back in time to the morning. The alternative was to question this reality in entirety, to wonder if she'd been knocked over by a car and was currently living out some sort of coma dream.

Maddie went inside to find Mrs H in the hallway, her hand guiltily frozen over the heating thermostat.

"I was just checking it," she said.

"Knock yourself out," said Maddie and went through to the living room. The local news had cycled round again.

"*—Waris Technical will begin construction of a new*

engineering facility near the town of Wirkswell. The engineering company is expected to—"

"To bring up to five hundred jobs to the regional economy," Maddie said in sync with the news reader.

Kevin looked round at her and frowned. "Do you not like me calling you a Bobby Dazzler?" he said.

She frowned back, then understood he was referring to her clothes. "I'm just getting changed again," she said.

She went upstairs to her bedroom. There on the bed were the clothes she'd laid out for the gig this evening, the ripped T-shirt and jeans, still ripped, no longer repaired and then disastrously re-ripped.

"Why have I travelled back in time?" she said to herself and then, "*How* have I travelled back in time?"

She tried to envisage it in her own mind. If she did nothing, the other version of herself would go to work, meet Gregory at lunch, put on a disastrous outfit, pick up a disastrously over-polished bass before going to a total calamity of a gig, then step into a men's toilet cubicle and travel back in time.

"A toilet time machine?" she mused.

The point was, that by tonight, her earlier self would be gone, travelled back in time and she, the one who had already travelled, would be able to continue with her own life. She just needed to stay out the way of her earlier self for the duration of the day. She wasn't sure what would happen if she saw her earlier self, or worse still actually make physical contact. For some reason she couldn't rationalise, she pictured two Maddies occupying the same space as horribly disastrous, like – *BOOM!* – thermonuclear matter/anti-matter explosion disastrous.

She needed to stay out of her own way and simply do nothing with her day…

"Or…"

She picked up a pad of post-its on her bedside which she used to write song ideas and midnight notes to herself. On one, she wrote *DO NOT MEND THESE!* and placed it plainly on her ripped jeans. She stuck *DO NOT OPEN* on the case of her bass. To be doubly sure she opened the case and stuck *DO NOT POLISH THIS GUITAR* on the instrument itself.

She stepped back and thought. Her diary was in her coat pocket. Today's list read:

WASHING

Mrs H

Work

Greg – weed

Chippy

Drying

Gig @ 7

SHE COULD MAKE sure that her earlier self successfully did all of these. In fact, she could do all the things she should have done as well. From her bedside cabinet, she grabbed the Alice's Demons flyers that Flynn's mate had printed up. She could give her earlier self a helping hand and maybe drum up some support for the evening.

With a fresh farewell for Kevin and Mrs H, she headed out towards Wirkswell town centre, safe in the knowledge that her earlier self was in the office and off the streets. She walked up and down the pedestrianised high street several times, handing out leaflets to anyone who looked young enough to possibly enjoy the heavy metal outpourings of Alice's Demons. In truth, there seemed to be very few such people in Wirkswell, a town which seemed to specialise in hunch-shouldered old ladies and careworn and blank-eyed old men.

Not feeling her pile going down at all, she decided to head round to Market Street and try her luck there. There was row of parked cars on both sides of the road and Maddie began placing a flyer under the windscreen wiper of each car. Were the cars more likely to belong to younger music fans? No. But she was already bored with trying to hand them out.

A small red car pulled into a nearby bay and a woman stepped out. The woman was slender and her clear, almost beautiful facial features made it hard to tell where in the great landscape of middle age she belonged. Maddie would have not recognised her, would have ignored her completely, if she hadn't spoken with her and about her yesterday – well, earlier today – well, later today, but in a different timeline.

"Astrid Bohart."

The woman looked at her sharply. "Did you say something?"

"Um," said Maddie. She looked and saw that, yes, the car was a Skoda CitiGo and Astrid had just parked and was looking at her phone, possibly trying to buy time on the parking app.

"You're not in that zone," said Maddie, pointing at the sign across the road.

"Pardon?"

"You're going to buy a ticket for zone one-seven-two-six but it's the wrong zone."

"I can see what zone I'm in," the woman snapped.

The memories were all coming flooding back. Mrs Bohart had taught young Maddie Waites History at Wirkswell Secondary High. Back then, Maddie had found the woman terrifyingly strict and humourless, and she was one of the reasons Maddie had definitely not chosen History as one of her GCSE options. Which was all a shame really because Maddie had loved History, had specifically loved the *Horrible Histories* books and TV show, but whatever fun and joy the *Horrible Histories* had brought to the subject, Astrid Bohart sucked it right out again.

"I'm saying that, if you park here and buy that ticket, you'll get a ticket. I mean you'll get a Parking Charge Notice."

Astrid studied her through narrowed eyes, taking in her appearance. "You're not the traffic warden."

"I am not the traffic warden," said Maddie.

"Why are you threatening me with a ticket? Is this some sort of scam?"

"For fuck's sake, miss, I'm not threatening—"

Astrid tapped her phone. "Done."

"But it's the wrong sodding ticket."

The woman turned towards the nearest shop. It was a grubby looking newsagents beneath an equally grubby looking colonnade walkway. Above the newsagent sign was a temporary sagging sign that did indeed declare that the shop sold fireworks.

"I'm only going to be five minutes," she said primly.

"But they'll ticket you!"

"Hardly!" said Astrid and was gone.

Maddie sighed and worked her way along to the end of the row where a civil parking enforcement officer had just pulled up on his moped. He dismounted and lifted his helmet advisor.

"Could you do me a favour and not give a ticket to that red Skoda?" said Maddie.

The enforcement officer sniffed. "What's wrong with the red Skoda?"

"Nothing. She's just bought a ticket for the wrong zone. I told her. I'm with the council." She began to pat herself for her council ID, but in this timeline it was around the neck of her earlier self at the office.

"I'll take a look," the officer said and began sauntering over to Astrid's car.

"I said *don't* give her a ticket," Maddie shouted after him, but he just gave a lazy wave without looking back and sauntered on.

"Shit," she whispered.

Reckoning she had done about as much damage as she could do here, Maddie retreated.

Walking on, she realised this time travel business was hard. To have any slight knowledge of the events which had gone before added extra complexity and headaches. As a woman, she knew perfectly well what it was like to be able to see what others could not, but then be completely ignored when she tried to point it out. But she had an inkling time travel added a whole new level of annoyance.

Perhaps it would be best if she steered clear of earlier Maddie's business and just focus on getting her own timeline back on track.

Maddie's feet were taking her towards the Old Schoolhouse bar before she knew it. That had been the scene of her time travel jaunt. If she could somehow reverse it, pop back to the future and just get out of her earlier self's hair, that would be ideal.

The Old Schoolhouse opened up at lunchtime. It functioned as a low-quality café bar for much of the day. They had a food menu mostly consisting of ham sandwiches, cheese sandwiches, and ham and cheese sandwiches. When Maddie asked the woman serving what the salad garnish was, she told her it was crisps – either prawn cocktail or smoky bacon.

Maddie sat in the bar, which had been the little assembly hall back in the days when this had been a school, and ate a cheese sandwich and prawn cocktail crisps. Then, when she felt the place was quiet enough, she went out into the back corridor and into the gents toilet. It was the far cubicle on the right she'd been in when the light changed and she'd been whisked back to the morning.

"I stepped inside and closed the door." She turned the latch to lock herself in. "And then I stood here and..."

And what? What had she done? She'd done nothing. She'd stood here and waited for the men to stop pissing, and then it had happened. But that couldn't just be it. If this toilet cubicle was a time machine – and she recognised how stupid that sounded – then it wouldn't just send everybody who stood in it back in time. She must had done *something*.

She rattled the door. She knocked on it. She loudly declared "Go go, time machine!" She tapped the tiles on the floor in case one of them was a secret button. She waggled the toilet handle until it went the wrong way and something inside snapped.

The toilet began to flush.

She banged on the side panels. She stood really still in case the key was stillness. But none of it seemed to be working.

The toilet was still flushing. In fact, the bowl was filling up. She reflexively pressed the handle again to see if I would stop. The handle spun limply.

"Oh, crap," she said and unbolted the door just as the water crested the lip of the bowl. She stumbled back away from the rising cascade and, recognising this was no longer a good place to be, hurried out. The pool of water was expanding across the tiles as she shut the door to the gents behind her.

She'd broken the time machine.

7

Maddie was strongly tempted to tell the woman at the bar there was a flood in the gents toilet, but couldn't work out how she'd phrase it without revealing she had been in there. She decided to leave it for someone else to discover.

She went outside and found a wall to sit on. Travelling forwards to her own proper time was not a thing. She only had another five or six hours to wait before her earlier self vanished into the past anyway. So she waited.

Evening descended and the early birds turned up for the band night at the Old Schoolhouse. Maddie watched them go in.

When she saw the neckbeard setting up his little ticket table at the front door, she walked over. "Krist Novoselic," she said.

"What?"

"The bassist in Nirvana. Krist Novoselic. Along with Kurt

Cobain – lead vocals and guitar – he was the only member of Nirvana who was in the band beginning to end. The drummer most people associate with the band is Dave Grohl, although he was like the fifth or sixth drummer they had."

Neckbeard's face screwed up in disdainful confusion.

"When you next see me come in, don't ask me none of your rock trivia shite," she said. "I'm Maddie Waites, bassist with Alice's Demons, and I'll be playing tonight."

Before he could say anything, Maddie turned away and went back to her spot on the wall to watch and wait.

The first bands were turning up, and she heard their sound checks from inside. Then saw her younger self again, coming up the hill. Her younger self still had that hunched and downcast air about her. Maddie straightened her back and held her head high. She really must try to do something about that slouch.

Posture aside, Maddie was pleased to see that her younger self was now a full half hour earlier than she herself had been and was wearing the ripped jeans and T-shirt which she'd originally intended to wear. On time and properly prepared. Not bad. Maddie considered her own disastrous blanket kilt and leggings effort and wondered what on earth she'd been thinking.

The first band began to play.

"Job done," she told herself. All she needed to do now was wait for the gig to reach its triumphant climax and for earlier Maddie to go back in time when she went in search of Gregory— "Huh?"

Gregory was coming out of the bar and crossing the road in a stiff-legged, hopping skip. This didn't happen last time.

She rushed over to intercept him. “Where are you going?”

He stared at her, surprised. “I’ve just got to find a toilet.” He looked her up and down. “Did you change?”

“Never mind that. You’re due on any minute.”

“I ... I’m not feeling good. I need a loo.”

“The toilets are in there,” she said and pointed.

“Out of order,” he said. “Big sign on the door saying wet floor. Someone—”

“Broke the toilet,” she groaned.

There was a musical bum squeak from his trousers. “Gotta go,” he grunted and dashed off, arse cheeks clenched.

Maddie looked round. As evening fell, there were few places still open. She could see a corner shop and a Chinese takeaway, neither of which would offer toilet facilities to a desperate drummer.

She looked to the converted church and tried to think. Without their drummer, could Alice’s Demons go on stage? If they didn’t go on, would earlier Maddie lose Gregory’s weed? If there was no Gregory and no stolen weed, would earlier Maddie have any reason to step inside the Time Toilet?

At first Maddie was gripped by the fear that she and earlier Maddie would be here together forever; that there would now and for all time be two Maddies in this timeline. She was then gripped by the chilling thought if the other Maddie didn’t go back in time, would she herself simply cease to exist. If there was no time travel, then she wouldn’t be here. But if she hadn’t gone back in time and broken the toilet, Gregory wouldn’t have had to leave and then—

The possibilities – none of them good – flip-flopped back

and forth in her mind. Whatever the truth of the matter, she needed to fix things.

She rushed to the Old Schoolhouse entrance.

"Six quid in. What band are you here to see?" said Neckbeard.

"I'm the drummer in Alice's Demons," she said automatically, giving voice to a half-baked idea before she'd even properly formulated it in her own mind.

He pulled back, recognising her. "You said you're the bassist."

"I was. I am. Well, no, that was earlier me." She cleared her throat. "My twin sister. My earlier ... older ... twin sister. She's bass. I'm drums."

Before he could question this, she pushed in. She had decided to offer her own competent services as a drummer and replace Gregory without thinking, but she couldn't go up on stage and simply present herself. Other Maddie would recognise her instantly, and wouldn't swallow the other twin nonsense for a moment.

The band on stage was thrashing its way through their final number. Maddie cast about. She need a disguise. She was imagining something like a luchador wrestling mask, although there was never a luchador around when you needed one. Over at one table there was what looked like a long crimson scarf draped over the back of a woman's chair. It looked like the kind of thing that could be wrapped around a head several times and still give enough space for a person to breathe.

It was an awful idea, and it was also all she had. The band were milking the last of the audience's goodwill with some drawn out closing chords and a wildly uncontrolled drum solo. Maddie hurried to the table and grabbed the scarf, opening her mouth to offer some pleas and thank yous when a hand gripped her arm.

"Ah ha!"

Maddie turned. In the pink and blue half-light it took her a moment to realise the hand belonged to Astrid Bohart.

"Didn't think I'd find you?" spat the miserable ex-teacher.

"Huh?"

Adjusting the small rucksack on her back, Astrid waved a creased and damp flyer for Alice's Demons in her face. "You don't get to shop me to the traffic wardens and get away with it. What did you want? Money? Is this a prank of some sort?"

"Please, Miss Bohart, I don't have time for this."

With her free hand, she grabbed the scarf from the chair. The other end was under the backside of the woman it belonged to. The woman looked round sharply.

"Sorry. I need a mask," said Maddie.

"The warden gave me a ticket," said Astrid. "And when I phoned the council to complain who should I happen to speak to, eh?"

On stage, the singer cleared his throat. "As many of you might know, our roadie and friend, Skid, died earlier this week. He took a corner too fast on his bike and he went into a, well, a skid…"

"Oh, you might have pretended you didn't know who I was," Astrid hissed at Maddie, "but it was you."

Two people nearby shushed at them harshly while the singer stumbled with his sombre words.

"You're not having my scarf," said the woman still sitting on it.

"You are going to pay my fine for me and I will be making an official complaint," said Astrid.

"Please, Miss Bohart," said Maddie, trying to pull away from Astrid and claim the scarf at the same time.

"Bohart?" said a tall man with a soul patch just to the side. "Druggie Bohart? Fuck! Dylan, look. Druggy Bohart." The man was doing the universal mime of someone smoking a joint.

"I did not do drugs!" Astrid snapped.

"That piece of road is notorious and we all know Skid liked to live fast," the singer was saying.

Around Maddie and Astrid there was an angry mood amongst people who had more respected for the departed  Skid than either of them apparently did. The woman with the scarf stood up to remonstrate with Maddie, releasing the scarf from under her, and Maddie went reeling back. Astrid did not go with her. Angry hands were pulling her another way by her rucksack.

A cheery chant of "Druggy Bohart, druggy druggy Bohart," was starting up among a handful of people.

"Anyway, the funeral's a week on Tuesday," continued the singer, as distracted as everyone else by the ruckus in the corner.

There was a high ripping sound of a backpack zipper breaking open, and several tubes fell to the ground.

"She's got her gear," someone laughed drunkenly.

"They're mine!" Astrid shouted.

Maddie could see Neckbeard and a bouncer pushing through the crowd towards them.

"Look at these!" someone shouted and there was the flicker of cigarette lighter.

Maddie recognised that those large tubes were definitely not cannabis joints, and very definitely not something a sane and sober person would light indoors.

With a soft but powerful *FOOM*, the first incandescent star from a Roman Candle shot up into the rafters of the hall. Half the crowd could not resist the urge to go "Ooh!" or "Aah!" in wonder. By the time the second firework lifted off from Soul Patch's hand, many of the crowd had realised it wasn't such a great idea to be indoors near powerful pyrotechnics.

"That's mine!" Astrid yelled. "They're mine! You can't have them!"

Maddie stumbled away, released from Astrid's grip. The crowd was moving into full scale panic mode. There was a press towards the door. The band on stage had left. Maddie wheeled round and saw, at the edge of the stage, Flynn and her younger self (unpolished black bass in hand, Maddie noted). They were both staring directly at her.

A pink firework ball of flame shot towards the stage and put a neat hole straight through the bass drum. Shouts and what were building up to be screams filled the air. Maddie wished none of this had ever happened, then someone big and clumsy collided with her back and she was flung against a round table that flipped and collapsed under her weight and suddenly the light was very bright.

8

Maddie closed her eyes automatically as she fell hard against the table, only opening them again when she realised everything around her was suddenly very quiet. She looked about. The table she'd fallen on was no longer there. It, like the other tables, was pushed up against the wall. Gone were the drinkers and the drinks and the fireworks. Daylight came in from the high Victorian school hall windows. It was once again the light of morning.

She rolled into a sitting position. She still had the woman's long red scarf in her hand.

Already suspecting what it would say, she took her phone from her pocket and looked at the time. The screen glitched for a moment before settling down. The date was Friday. The time was seven a.m. She'd gone back in time again.

"Some fucking Groundhog Day shit," she seethed and pushed herself to her feet, stuffing the scarf in her pocket.

She knew the main doors would be locked so went round to the fire exit and barged her way out onto the side steps. As the cold air of morning hit her, she was also struck by the fear she might bump into her previous self – time traveller number one on her first loop round. But with the time toilet broken, that shouldn't be possible—

Except she hadn't time-travelled in the toilet cubicle this time. She'd done it openly on the dance floor. So, it wasn't a toilet time machine. It was something else... She patted herself as though expecting to find something revealing on her.

"Maybe it's me," she said to no one. "Maybe I've got the power."

But why now? That didn't make sense. Unless it was like something she'd had to grow into; like some sort of very late puberty time-travel.

With an irritated huff, she began to walk down into the town.

"Mornin'," said a postie, coming up the pavement.

Maddie twirled as she let him past. "Er, morning."

This was her third time living this day. The first time had been a disaster. The second time had been an equal disaster. She needed to make this time work and then just get on with her life.

She wanted to call herself, but couldn't phone her own number because she would be phoning the very phone she was holding in her hands right now. She wasn't even sure how the telecommunications network was coping with two identical phones in existence at the same time. Maybe that was what was causing the occasional *No Service* message appearing on her screen.

She called her home landline. There was a possibility Uncle Kevin might pick up, but the man's selective deafness also applied to ringing phones and other alarms.

"Hello," said a voice. Her voice.

Maddie froze for a moment. What could she say? She certainly couldn't use her own voice. She went for something that she immediately felt was cartoonishly nasal.

"Oh, hello. This is Kirsty Applejack from the council. The council offices are closed for the day."

"Oh?" said other Maddie.

"Yes. We've had an asbestos leak and we need to assess it."

"Leak?"

Maddie winced. "Yes, leak. So, we're asking employees to stay at home today."

"Oh, right. Do I need to do... anything?"

"No, no. Stay at home. Don't contact anyone at the council because it's all closed. Maybe you've got ... got a special event or something to practise for." Maddie rolled her eyes at herself.

"Pardon?" said her clueless twenty-four hours younger self.

"I thought I heard you were in a band. Special gig tonight."

"Oh. We do. Didn't know we were famous."

"You need to practise. Anyway. Stay at home. Get ready for the gig. Do not come into work."

"Because of the asbestos leak?"

"Exactly," said Maddie and ended the call.

That had actually gone better than she'd expected. She had made her earlier self stay at home where she could practise the songs and guard her clothes against Mrs Hawkshaw. Meanwhile, Maddie could go to work and cover for herself.

The walk from the Old Schoolhouse to Wirkswell town hall took her down some rarely taken roads. When she passed an Acacia Drive, the street sign struck her as oddly familiar. Rather than wonder where she'd seen it before, she wondered if she was going to be getting a lot of déjà vu as a time traveller; as though the accumulation of her selves occupying the same timeline would somehow trigger some greater awareness of what was going down.

Then she realised the truth was much more prosaic. She had seen the words on a computer screen two days – well, later today, two versions back.

"Astrid Bohart."

Maddie hurried into the crescent. It was still early. She wasn't due in work just yet, which meant Astrid had not yet parked up and got a ticket, which might lead the angry ex-teacher and ex-pothead to come along and sabotage the gig.

Yes! Maddie saw a little red car parked in a driveway and, yes, that was the right registration number.

"All I've got to do is stop the car parking there," she told herself.

The CitiGo was parked in front of a garage door. The house curtains were drawn and the place seemed entirely quiet. Three doors nearer to, there was a builder's skip in the driveway: rubble and remains from a porch extension that had yet to be completed. Maddie stood on tiptoe and rooted through the end of the skip. She didn't know what she was looking for, but she'd know it when she saw it. She considered and rejected a carpet gripper, a broken hammer and a shard of glass before settling on a long bent carpentry nail.

She approached Astrid's house, fighting the temptation to approach in a stealthy crouch which would have undoubtedly looked more suspicious that just walking. She stopped behind the CitiGo. She initially thought of propping the nail up between ground and tyre so it would puncture the tyre as the vehicle rolled back, but that felt overly complex. She should just do it. With real but minimal regret, she found a deep groove in the tyre and pushed until her thumbs were white and bloodless. The nail slipped in and the tyre began to hiss.

"Job done." She said it to reassure herself.

There was a loud bang and a high-pitched yelp of distress from within the house. Maddie stood up swiftly, staring. There was no follow up noise which made the bang and scream seem immediately more serious.

The normal thing to do was just to walk away. It was absolutely the normal thing to do after sabotaging Astrid's car, Maddie told herself. Walk away. There were plenty of reasons why something had popped or exploded in the house. She should walk away.

She didn't.

Maddie walked carefully to the open gate by the side of the house. She could just find a window, peek in and when she saw movement, know that everything was okay and leave again. That was all. There was a boxy white CCTV camera on the side of house. She looked at it. It looked at her. It didn't move. There was no light. It looked dead.

She moved on. There was a small square window in the side of the garage, Maddie moved closer and peered in. There was a light on and wisps of smoke filled the air. The rest of the room was not particularly comprehensible. The far wall was lined with shelves crammed with boxes and folders, and enough tools for a significant workshop. In front of that was a large table, as big as a snooker table, but covered with lumpy and even scatterings of sand. In the middle of that stood a smoking and blast-damaged contraption, cylindrical yet angular, spindly yet robust.

Astrid Bohart wafted away smoke then lowered the goggles on her forehead. Through the window, Maddie heard her say something like "Burned too quickly. Need regular gunpowder."

"What the fuck?" Maddie whispered.

What was the crazy bitch doing? Setting off fireworks in her own garage? But that thing on the sandy table. It looked like a home science project. Home science project plus gunpowder equals...

"She's a fucking terrorist."

Astrid couldn't have heard her but she looked up regardless. Their eyes met. Surprise shifted almost immediately to anger.

"Balls," said Maddie.

Astrid came rushing round the table. Maddie legged it, down the drive and away along Acacia Crescent.

9

Maddie would have run all the way into town, but she got stitch in her side after a hundred metres and slowed down to a panicked walk. She still had the crimson scarf from last night. She wound that round her lower face to disguise herself a little. She'd have wrapped the rest of it round her like some sort of niqab/hijab/thing, but firstly, didn't know how to and secondly, worried that it was probably racially not cool.

On speedy fearful legs, she got to the town hall and swiped in twenty minutes early. She was in her draughty office moments earlier than the first of her colleagues but not so early that she could sit down before they noticed her less than informal attire.

Tracy Taylor-Thomson looked at Maddie's dog blanket skirt.

"Is that a ... a kilt?" she hazarded.

"Yes!" said Maddie, gratefully. "Yes it is."

"I didn't know you were Scottish."

"Och, aye," said Maddie, immediately thinking bad Scottish impressions were probably as racially insensitive as impromptu hijabs. She didn't have enough brain power to work it out right now. She had just witnessed a domestic terrorist preparing for something and she was living through her third version of the same day without a wink of sleep in between.

"I suspect someone has been out late and not had time to change," suggested Monica McMahon.

"Oh, those were the days. To be young, free and single."

"Yes. Yes, that," said Maddie, putting in her earphones and logging on to work.

The morning was quiet. There were no emergencies and, critically, no call from Astrid Bohart. She checked the parking database intermittently. There was no parking charge notice for the little red CitiGo. She wondered if she should call the police and tell them that there was a bomb-maker in Acacia Crescent. She googled anonymous police tip-off lines and still didn't know what to do.

The greatest danger she faced that morning was falling asleep. That and hunger. Her mind tumbled from thoughts of hunger, to the idea of getting a Gregg's sausage roll, to the one she'd had two days before, to her lunchtime rendezvous with Gregory.

"Shit," she said, standing up involuntarily.

The women in the Amenities and Facilities office stared at her.

"I ... need a shit," she told them and left.

She called Gregory as she made her way down the stairs. "You want to meet up at lunch time," she said to him.

"You said you were at home," he said. *"I'm heading over now—"*

"I'm in town. How soon can you get to Alice's place?"

"Two minutes."

And he was true to his word. He was in the windy courtyard behind Wirkswell Museum in no time at all. He had his parka pulled up against the cold.

"I thought you were working from home. An asbestos leak or something."

"False alarm," she said.

"You know asbestos doesn't leak, don't you? It just ... exists."

"Whatever. You've got something for me. Hand it over." She didn't mean to sound rushed, but Gregory was now just another box she needed to tick off today.

"You okay?" he said. He took out a spliff and was putting it to his lips to light it for her.

"Do not smoke that," she said. "It gives you the shits."

"Sometimes."

"Today it will. I need you on top form for the gig tonight."

Gregory's handsome eyes narrowed at her. "You're not normally this passionate about the band."

"Maybe this is one of my passionate days." She snatched the spliff from him. "Now give me the weed."

He paused with his hand in his pocket. "How did you know that?"

She shrugged. "Heard rumours about some spectacularly

high foxes on the allotments. I put two and two together. Your mum is getting suspicious."

He took the wrapped wad of weed from his pocket and slapped it into her hand. "Those foxes. So high. Like they were flying through altered dimensions."

"I'm sure they valued the experience."

He waggled a finger at her blanket and leggings combo. "This a new look you're going for."

She thought about her earlier self, hopefully practising at home. "I'll probably wear something more conventional later."

"Nah, I like this," he said.

"I'm so glad I need your approval."

He did a minimal bow. "Touché, madam."

She went and bought three sausage rolls from Gregg's and scoffed two of them on the walk back to the office. She was now fed, which only compounded her other most immediate complaint. Maddie went into the town hall toilets, sat on the loo and, without intending to but knowing exactly what she was going to do, fell asleep with her face against the cubicle wall.

She woke and looked at her phone. She was surprised to discover she had slept for three hours in that position. Time travel of a different sort in a different toilet. She ran the water in the basin and washed her face to wake herself up. There was a red mark, sort of like the imprint of an iron, where she'd leant against the wall. No amount of rubbing seemed to make it go away.

"Ah, she returns," said Tracy Taylor-Thomson when Maddie reappeared in the office.

"I got called out," said Maddie. "Work stuff."

"We heard the snoring," said Monica McMahon.

Maddie said nothing and blushed. At least for a moment, her two red cheeks might match.

At the end of the day, with no home of her own to go to, she loitered in town, ate the third sausage roll, and wandered very slowly up to the Old Schoolhouse.

She hadn't yet decided if there were currently one or two of her earlier selves at loose in the town. She'd not seen more than one. And if they were stacking up, one of top of the other, if she travelled back in time again, would the fourth one already be here?

She kept a low profile, found a different wall to skulk by, and watched the entrance to the club.

The newest and entirely oblivious Maddie came up the hill in good time, bass in hand, dressed in ripped jeans and T-shirt. Good.

The first band started their sound check and more people arrived. With no further evidence available from outside, she could do nowt but assume all was going well. She was beginning to feel a little more relaxed when she saw Gregory striding away from the old school.

She hesitated only a second, then crossed the road to intercept him. "Gregory!"

He stopped and turned. His eyes widened, first in anger and then surprise.

"How ... how did you get out here?" He pointed at her clothes. "You're different again."

She ignored the questions. "The gig's about to start. Our gig."

He scoffed violently. “You think this is funny?”

“What’s funny?”

“Oh, playing super coy now!” His whole body was tensed with emotion. “Friendship means you don’t get to agree to hold a significant quantity of weed from someone and then pretend you know nothing about it.”

“Ah—”

“Ah? Fucking *Ah*?” He seethed. “A joke’s a joke, but you don’t then accuse me of being a psycho, make out you’re the one angry at me. I made you a friendship bracelet, I did. I know it’s a bit immature but—”

He stopped. His eyes were on Maddie’s wrist and the friendship bracelet he’d given her two iterations ago. He dipped in his pocket and came out with an identical friendship bracelet, strands of woven wool with cube letters threaded onto it.

“How…?”

Maddie backed away, cradling her friendship bracelet. “They can’t touch. Two identical things can’t occupy the same space, can they?”

“What?”

“It’s like matter and anti-matter, isn’t it?”

“What?”

There was a momentary whoop and only then did Maddie see the police car that was coming along the street beside them.

10

"Go back inside," said Maddie. "Quickly."

The police car stopped beside them.

Gregory looked at her.

"I'm still carrying it," she said.

He frowned.

"The *weed*!" she hissed.

His eyes went wide, then, split-second decision made, turned and walked nonchalantly away, back towards the bar.

Maddie made to go the other away.

"Excuse me, miss," said the police officer in the doorway of his car.

She looked at him as innocently as she could. "Yes?"

The other officer got out. They were broad men. Big. Probably not very fast but they were big.

"Can you tell me your name?" said one.

"Am I legally required to do so?" she said automatically.

The nearest one held a piece of folded paper in his hand. He looked at it then looked at Maddie. "It's her," he said.

"Who is who?" said Maddie.

"Where were you at eight thirty this morning, miss?"

She shrugged. "At home. Making breakfast for my Uncle Kevin. He'll be wondering where I am."

He held out the folded sheet. It was a cheaply printed picture, from a definitely functioning CCTV camera. Maddie Waites' face looked up gormlessly straight into the camera.

"Ah."

"I'll take that as admission of guilt, Brad," said the other officer.

Maddie considered legging it but it was already too late. She had barely turned when the copper took hold of his arm.

"Maddie Waites, I am arresting you on suspicion of causing criminal damage—"

"I didn't— Wait! How do you know my name?"

"Someone dropped a flyer in the driveway, didn't they, miss?" said the cop as his grip moved to her wrists. "Your band has a lovely and informative Instagram page."

"Shit!"

"You have the right to remain silent but anything you do say—"

"Wait. You can't do this. She can't snitch on me to the police."

"Who?"

"Mrs Bohart. Astrid."

"Got that, Brad?"

"Camera's on and recording, Rick."

"Anything you do say may be used in evidence against you."

"But she's a terrorist!" said Maddie.

He secured a cable tie around her wrists with a loud, high-pitched *scritch*.

"She's a what?" said the other officer, chortling.

"A terrorist! A bomb-maker! Her garage is full of explosives!"

Officers Brad and Rick looked at each other.

"Are you telling us the truth, Maddie? We take a very dim view of people who lie to us. Particularly about terrorism."

"Lying about terrorism is bad," the other confirmed.

"I am telling you the truth!" she said.

They looked at each other again. There was much sighing. It was sort of the sighing Maddie suspected was more about the extra paperwork she was creating for them than anything else.

Maddie was put in the back of the police car and they drove off towards Acacia Crescent. It had felt right to tell them, that somehow exposing a mad bomb-maker would counteract the very small matter of puncturing Astrid's tyres, and yet... As the car wended its way through the evening streets, she couldn't quite work out how this situation, right now, was going to be in any better than if she'd just shut her mouth.

The car pulled up outside Astrid's house. There was the CitiGo on the driveway, still with a flat tyre. Officer Brad turned to look at Maddie.

"We're going to go and chat with Mrs Bohart. You are

going to sit there very quietly. This car is very solid and you can't break anything."

"And don't even think of doing a dirty protest on the back seat," added Officer Rick. "It'll be worse for you cos you're the one who'll have to sit in it. I speak from experience." He exchanged a glance with Brad. "I mean experienced other people who did it, not that *I* did it. Why would I—?"

"Come on," said Brad and got out.

The doors locked with a chunky *thunk*. Maddie wasn't going to break out of the back of a police car.

She watched them go up to the house. They rang the doorbell and a light came on from within. There was talking on the doorstep, inaudible from within the car, and much pointing. There were gestures at the garage and then there was waving of arms and the discussion became much more animated.

Astrid Bohart stepped out and walked to the garage door. It was unlocked and opened. The police took a step inside. Astrid clearly objected to this. There was much more arm waving, then shouting which Maddie could hear, even though the words were indistinct. One of the officers picked up a backpack. Astrid snatched it from him and, abruptly, it was Astrid Bohart who was cuffed with cable ties and being marched over to the police car.

"No, don't bring her here!" said Maddie.

But that was exactly what was happening. Maddie shuffled over and Officer Rick sat Astrid in the rear seat, guiding her head so she didn't clout herself on the ceiling. The backpack was shoved at her feet. The door shut and

Astrid turned to look at Maddie. The woman's eyes were wild, livid, animalistic.

"What in God's name did you tell them?" she spat.

Maddie opened her mouth to speak, but only an embarrassed wheeze came out. "I was trying to help, honest, Mrs Bohart."

"Do I know you?"

"I mean, you don't but you did. I'm Maddie Waites. Honestly, I was trying to stop you getting a parking ticket."

"By calling the police?"

"Well, not that bit. I only told them because you sent them to arrest me."

"You attacked my car."

"To stop you getting a ticket."

"What ticket? Are you deranged?"

"It's complicated."

"It's complicated?" said Astrid, bound fists clenched. "You attack me and then get the police to—" She put her mouth to the window and yelled. "Don't touch that! That's mine! You can't touch that!"

The police were manhandling the boxy, spindly cylinder thing just inside the garage.

"That's not a real bomb, is it?" asked Maddie.

"What? That's the LM-5 Eagle lander, obviously. You—" she whirled on Maddie "—you work for them, don't you?"

"Who?"

"Them! *Them*!" It seemed that with each utterance, Astrid was trying to imbue the word with greater meaning. "Yes. That makes sense. You're here to bring me down, take me in. I bet you're wearing a wire, aren't you?"

Astrid was now turning round grabbing at Maddie's coat with her tied hands.

"Get off!" Maddie tried to fight her off.

"Frightened of something, huh?"

Astrid had hold of her now, was crawling across to her side of the seat. There was a hand in her pockets. "Ha! What's this?"

"No, not that," said Maddie.

Astrid had the block of weed and was holding it up. Maddie glanced towards the garage. One of the cops was on the radio. The other was hurrying towards the commotion in the car.

"Sent to plant things on me again!"

"We can't let them see this!" said Maddie, fighting the thin but strong older woman for control of the weed.

The cop was almost at the car. This day was turning out worse than any of the others. Much worse. The car door opened.

Suddenly, the car vanished and everything was bright piercing light.

11

It had started out as an ordinary day for Astrid Bohart, but had gone rapidly downhill from there.

She'd risen early, checked her e-mails and then sat down to a bowl of cornflakes – Kellogg's, because those were the best ones. She then rechecked her mails and phoned the two local recruitment agencies she was signed up with to ascertain if there was going to be any teaching supply work for her that day. There was not.

It was a day for herself then. She spent some time with the lunar lander in the garage, and was doing a run-through of the landing with the camera filming when the gunpowder charge for the lander unit burned through too quickly and exploded, destroying one side of the lander. As she was wafting away the fumes she had seen the face of an intruder at the window and given chase, only to discover that the horrible oik had stuck a nail in her rear tyre.

There was simply no understanding some people, really.

The day's plans had to change again. Instead of driving into town to get more fuel for the lander, she would have to walk. But not before she printed off a picture of the miscreant from the security software on her PC. The print-off and a damp flyer she'd found on the driveway were taken to Wirkswell police station. The young woman officer on the front desk seemed entirely uninterested in her complaint and bizarrely suggested that Astrid should phone the police.

"Why would I phone the police if I am literally talking to a police officer now?" Astrid had asked. "You are a police officer, are you not?"

The woman seemed to have lost her tongue by that point and Astrid asked to speak to her manager.

"The sergeant?" the officer had said.

"Is the sergeant your manager?"

"We don't call him that."

"Does he manage you? Does he tell you what to do?"

"I suppose so," the officer had said.

"Then he's your manager. I'll speak to him. Chop chop."

Astrid had given the sergeant the details of the crime and a piece of her mind beside, and did not leave until he had promised to put his "best officers" on it. Astrid had not been filled with hope, but left it at that.

And the rest of the day had returned to some sort of normality until late evening, when two bumbling policemen had turned up at her door, demanded to look in her garage and, within moments, she'd been handcuffed, had something about being arrested under the Explosive Substances Act 1883 mumbled at her, then found herself stuffed in the back of the police car alongside the tyre vandal:

a young, scruffy looking woman who appeared to be wearing a dog blanket for a skirt and then—

—had her ears popped in the violent transition?—

—she found herself sat on the road outside her own home and the bright light of early morning about her.

She sat there, gasping, the cold of the tarmac seeping into her buttocks. Her backpack was resting at her feet, but the police car had gone.

"Shit, not again," said the woman in the blanket-skirt.

Astrid looked at her. There was a compulsion to ask the young woman what she meant by 'again', but Astrid resisted it. She did not dance to other people's tunes.

She struggled to her feet, her hands still bound.

"You did this," she said. She looked at the suspicious dark block on the road. "You drugged me. You did this. It's..."

She looked around her. Everything looked as it should. This was her street. That was her house. That was her car (except now the rear tyre was no longer flat).

"Hallucinogenic drugs. Contact poison. They're getting clever."

"They?" said the young woman.

They. The FBI, CIA, MI5. The dark powers that were. The World Bank. The IMF. Even the Catholic Church. Astrid knew all about them.

"You work for them?" said Astrid.

"I work for Wirkswell council," the woman muttered. "I'm Maddie Waites. I'm sorry I did this to you."

"Ha! You admit it?"

The woman, Maddie, was tensing on her cable ties, trying unsuccessfully to pull them apart. "Yes. I did it. I didn't know I could do it to others too. Perhaps because we were touching."

"This is an assault upon my person!"

"I'm not sure that involuntary time travel counts as an assault."

"Time travel?"

The woman crouched by Astrid's front garden and tried rubbing the cable tie bonds against the low pebble-dashed walls. "It's Friday," she said. "Again. It's Friday morning."

"Poppycock."

The ties sprang apart and away with an audible snap.

"I'm going inside and calling the police," said Astrid and then frowned. "Again."

Maddie straightened her dog blanket skirt, readjusted the long crimson scarf around her neck and took out her phone.

"There! See?" she said, waving it unhelpfully in Astrid's face. "It's seven on Friday morning. This is the third – no fourth – time round for me." She flung at hand at Astrid's house. The curtains were drawn and the garage door was closed once more. "If you go in there, you will find another version of you, the version of you that hasn't travelled back in time. Don't touch her. I think you might destroy the universe or something."

Maddie turned towards the end of the street, appeared to rethink, and turned to face Astrid. "I am going to sit in Caruso's coffee shop – you know the one? – and drink something with fucking loads of caffeine in it. Maybe I will see you there."

With a humph and far more haughtiness than any young person had the right to possess, Maddie stomped down the crescent towards the town centre. A moment later, she hurried back, picked up the block of marijuana or whatever it was and stomped off again.

Astrid was still stunned – thoroughly understandable in the situation, she told herself – and simply watched the woman go before picking up her backpack and turning to her own house. Maddie had used the pebble-dashed wall and friction to cut her bonds. Astrid was not going to do the same. Astrid did not follow where others had led. She was a free thinker. Besides, rubbing oneself against a wall seemed uncouth.

She tried the front door of her house. It was locked. She went round to the side of the house and tried the back door. It was locked. She did not have her keys on her. They had been inside when the police had come calling. The previous owners had put a cat flap in the back door, and Astrid had long suspected that if she lay on the ground and reached through, she would be able to unlock the back door from the inside.

Except, her hands were currently tied together. There were scissors in the kitchen. But she needed to her hands free to access the kitchen and she needs the scissors in the kitchen to free her hands.

As this conundrum circled her mind, she realised there was someone in the house, looking out at her through the kitchen window. For more than a few seconds she wondered if it was some strange reflection in the window in the morning sun. And then the doppelganger moved. The false Astrid Bohart, wearing the T-shirt and dressing gown that

Astrid normally slept in, dropped the mug that Astrid had only drunk out of that morning.

"Who are you?" the false Astrid shouted.

"Who are you?" Astrid shouted back.

The false Astrid ran to the back door, not to open it but to check it was locked. "What do you want?" she yelled.

"You can't replace me!" Astrid shouted back. "I'll call the police!"

"Oh, you want me to call the police!"

The false Astrid came back into the kitchen. "Oh, yes, you want them to come here and have them install you here, instead of me."

Astrid paused. That was ... that was exactly what she wanted.

"I'm the real Astrid!" she shouted, trying to tap her chest expressively but only managing to punch her own chin with tied hands.

"That's just what a copy would say!" the false Astrid snarled. The false Astrid looked quite ugly when her face was screwed up in anger. Astrid hoped this was a mistake on the part of the manufacturers of this Stepford Wives version of herself.

The false Astrid was rummaging in the kitchen drawer. Astrid watched with interest and then alarm as the identity-stealing actor pulled out a chopping knife. It was the good one too, the one with the wooden handle and the surprisingly sharp blade. It would be the one Astrid would choose if she was going to fend off an attacker.

And now the woman was coming to the back door, murder clearly on her mind. She was armed, sure, but she wasn't dressed for combat. Then again, Astrid herself was hampered by her bound hands.

She decided that discretion was indeed the better part of valour and ran away. Further down the crescent, when she was sure the doppelganger was out of sight, Astrid leaned against a neighbour's wall and worked her cable ties against the sharp brick corner. It wasn't copying the young woman; it was entirely different class of wall.

12

Caruso's Coffee shop was on Baslow Road. The woman, Maddie, sat at a table in the window, sipping on a stupidly large bowl of frothy coffee and watching Astrid openly as she approached. Astrid made a point of going to the counter without looking at Maddie and placing her order before coming over to Maddie and sitting down.

"I used to teach a Maddie Waites," Astrid said.

"You certainly did," said Maddie.

Astrid nodded stiffly. "Made much of yourself?"

"A work in progress." There was an arrogance in the young woman's voice. "Done much since getting fired for smoking weed at school?"

"That was never proved."

"No smoke without fire."

"Smouldering," said Astrid.

"What?"

"Smouldering literally is smoke without fire."

"I was making a point."

"Poorly."

The waiter came over with a pot of tea for Astrid. She looked critically at the label of the tea bag hanging over the lip before dismissing him with a wave of her hand.

"If you must know," she said to Maddie, "I was framed."

"Do teachers get framed a lot?"

"I had written a paper on Phantom Time Hypothesis, a minor footnote on the theory, which had been accepted by a highly regarded website. Two days after publication, a partially smoked hand-rolled cigarette containing marijuana was found on my desk, along with this..."

She reached into her backpack, pushing aside the loose sparklers and bottle rockets that were in there and took out the poppet.

"What's that?" said Maddie.

Astrid thought it was plainly obvious. It was a lump of poorly carved wood, a crude child's dolly, a woman or girl with a lumpen head, a bump nose and only the vaguest suggestion of a lower body.

"This was a message," said Astrid.

Maddie, like an idiot, turned it over as though expecting to find an actual message on it somewhere.

"We're all puppets in the hands of the powers that be," Astrid pointed out.

"This and a joint and you think it was the government's doing?" said Maddie.

"Or whoever controls the government."

"Right, because of this Ghost Time Hypothesis—"

"Phantom Time Hypothesis."

Maddie took in a sharp, tired breath. "On any other day, I'm sure I'd want to hear about Phantom Time Hypothesis—"

"It's a revolutionary theory explaining why we have almost no archaeological data for much of what is called the Dark Ages and—"

"I said, on any other day," said Maddie.

Astrid was finding the girl to be unconscionably rude. Clearly education had not instilled this ... this *rock chick* with any kind of manners.

"I need to work out what to do," said Maddie. "I keep jumping through time."

"So, you say."

"Hey," Maddie said to the waiter. "What day is it?"

"It's Friday." He pointed at the digital time and date display on the TV screen in the corner.

"It's Friday," Maddie told Astrid. "Time travel. Got another explanation?"

Astrid looked at the street outside, the cars drifting by, the pedestrians going about their business.

"I've been transplanted to some mock-up of Wirkswell. A model town built by some alien power. I've seen *The Truman Show*," she said.

"And that seems more likely than time travel?"

Astrid gave it some thought. "Tell me your story," she said and, over additional drinks, Maddie did just that. Astrid listened and kept a mental note of questions she wanted to ask at the end.

"Does all marijuana cause your friend digestive problems?" was her first question. "Drug dealer would seem an odd career choice if it does."

"Um, I guess."

"And is his name really Thelonious?"

"Names may have been changed to protect the innocent."

"And the council really has the wrong parking zone signs put up on Market Street?"

"These are the questions you want to ask?" said Maddie.

Astrid pursed her lips. The child was impertinent, but also possibly correct. She thought further.

"You, ahem, travelled the first time while in a toilet cubicle at the school."

"I did."

"And the second time while in the hall there?"

"The bar. Yes."

"But the third time was at my house, last night."

"This night, actually. It's not happened yet."

Astrid nodded, ignoring Maddie's pedantry. "So, the geographical location seems irrelevant. It's not a time travelling toilet as you first assumed."

"I suppose not," Maddie agreed.

"The only common factor is you."

"It is."

"But you haven't time travelled before today?"

"No."

"So there's something different about you."

"Perhaps."

Astrid studied her. "Have you been in contact with a particle accelerator recently?" she hazarded.

"Where in Wirkswell would I find one of those?"

"Hmm. Are you menstruating?"

Maddie coughed on her coffee. "Fucking really? From particle accelerators to periods? That's your mental leap?"

"Considering the possibilities." Astrid looked her up and down. "You smoked marijuana. Drug induced altered states leading to temporal instability."

"Time weed?" said Maddie. "If every weed smoker went back in time, half of Wirkswell would have vanished long ago."

"Something about you has changed."

Maddie spread her arms. "This is me. This is my stuff. The scarf I picked up, but that was on my third rotation. The jacket's mine, my—"

"Why are you wearing a dog blanket?"

"It's a kilt."

"No, it isn't."

"I had to make some wardrobe decisions in a hurry. I've had this for years. Look, it's got Brownie badges on the other side. The only thing I picked up today before jumping back in time is—" she patted the bulge in her pocket "—the stuff Gregory – I mean Thelonious gave me and—"

She pulled back the cuff of her coat. There was a tatty bit of woven wool around her wrist with plastic cubes threaded on it. Astrid leaned forward to look at what was written on the cube letters.

"Mad, huh?" she said. She reached out to touch it, and a jolt of static electricity zapped her.

Maddie must have felt it too because she flinched. She frowned and touched it again.

"It's warm," she said. "Like proper warm."

"Mad," said Astrid.

13

A fox was sitting on the track leading up to the allotments and watching them.

"That fox is watching us," said Astrid.

"Foxes watch people," said Maddie.

"At two in the afternoon?"

The fox lifted its head to follow the flight of a bird overheard, and fell over.

"I think it might be high," said Maddie.

"High?"

She nodded. "Foxes round here are notoriously high."

That made no sense, but as no further answer was forthcoming from Astrid's ex-pupil she adjusted her backpack on her shoulder and they walked on.

"The allotments aren't officially in use," Maddie explained. "The council were going to repurpose them for something else."

"Do you mean sell them off to build houses?"

"In this instance, yes," said Maddie. "Not much else round here. Over there, it's all Burnley Manor land. So it's pretty quiet for Gregory to grow his crop. I mean Thelonious."

"You're not a very good liar," Astrid pointed out.

"Surely, that's a point in my favour."

There was a tall young man with an unwashed look about him standing in the gateway to the allotments. He had a smirk fixed to his face, but there was an astute inquisitiveness in his eyes. "Afternoon, Maddie."

"You look like you are expecting us," said Maddie.

"I knew you were coming."

"CCTV?"

"I have my ways," he said.

"Or long britches here could see us coming over the hedge," Astrid pointed out.

The chap, Gregory, looked at her pointedly. "Hello."

"Hello," said Astrid and didn't give him anything other than that.

Gregory made a vague hand gesture, perhaps marking out an imaginary object the size of the marijuana packet Maddie carried. "Is there a problem?" he said.

"No. No problem. All safe and fine," said Maddie. "Can I talk to you about friendship bracelets?"

There was a momentary alarm in his eyes. "Sure. You're aware it's just a friendship bracelet. You've not been reading too much into it."

Maddie frowned.

"Emotionally, I mean," he said.

"How would I read too much into it emotionally?"

"Like it meant something other than it did. Like I had special feelings or I was dying or something."

"Do you normally give friendship bracelets to people when you're dying?"

"I don't know. Yet."

Astrid had had enough of this playful pussyfooting around. "We want to know what's unusual about this friendship bracelet."

"Nothing," he said. "I just made it. Why?"

"Nothing unusual about its construction?" said Maddie. "No magic knots or—?"

"Magic knots?"

"Or...?"

He shook his head, his curls bouncing. "I just found some wool and had time to kill. Can't spend all day watching foxes giggling and falling over."

"Foxes don't giggle," said Astrid.

"On the inside they do."

"Wait. Found?" said Maddie.

"It is naturally foraged wool," said Gregory.

"Like from a sheep?"

"Okay, not that naturally. It's... Come see."

The lanky youth beckoned them to follow. The public allotments here had indeed been abandoned to the ravages of time. There were a number of abandoned and derelict sheds and greenhouses about the places. Strips of tattered polythene from ruined polytunnels fluttered in the wind like Buddhist prayer flags. Bamboo canes speared the earth in random places. The allotments were a battlefield on which time had won over humanity's attempts to bring order to the place.

"Almost anything I want can be found here," Gregory said. "I think I've cleared out most of the usable tools which have been left behind. I have strayed a little further afield." Suddenly he disappeared through the hedge via a gap Astrid hadn't noticed before. His head popped back out a second later. "Come on through."

Astrid squeezed through the gap after Maddie. She could not exactly say why she was spending the afternoon following a young beatnik who had both attacked her car and brought the police to her house, but it seemed this was exactly what she was doing.

Beyond the hedge was an orchard, bare of fruit at the moment.

"This is technically not my land," Gregory whispered as he crept in an exaggerated manner through the trees.

"As opposed to the allotment, which is?" asked Astrid at normal volume, refusing to play along with his pantomime.

"A different kind of ownership or lack thereof," he said, somewhat moodily. "It's here."

"What's here?" said Maddie.

He gestured with both hands. By a dilapidated shed someone had arranged a series of pallets into a box formation and was using it as a compost heap.

"Compost," said Maddie.

Gregory went to one end and stuck his hand in the leaf mulch, coming up with a scrap of wool, a single pale thread like a wiggling worm.

"It was in the compost," said Maddie.

Astrid moved closer. There were flecks and fragments of

wool on the surface and, as she dug in with her hands, slightly larger fragments of knitted material below. "Someone has shredded their knitting," she said. "Odd."

"What's odd is you sticking your hands in garden poo."

"It's compost, not manure," said Astrid.

"Same diff." Maddie turned to Gregory. "So you saw this and naturally thought, I'll make Maddie something out of this poop wool?"

"Recycling's good," he said.

"Got a bigger fragment here," said Astrid, carefully pulling free a section of knitting no bigger than the palm of her hand. It was a simple stitch, with white and red alternating to create a pattern of little stubby red crosses among the plain white. "I've seen this pattern before," she said, holding it up to the light.

Maddie stood next to her and looked at the ripped knitting. "Me too."

"Are you just saying that to feel included?" said Astrid.

"No, I have it's—"

"Alice's Demons," said Gregory.

"Pardon?" said Astrid.

He took out his phone, fiddled for a few seconds, then thrust it in her face. The screen contained an image of what appeared to be a music album cover. "It's our first EP. Self-recorded."

Under a title of *Alice's Demons* was a black and white woodcut image in a somewhat naïve style. In the centre was an image of a woman tied to a stake while individuals with belt-buckle hats and torches gathered round.

"The guy in the top left. His top looks the same, doesn't

it?" said Gregory. "Or maybe you were thinking of something else?"

"No, this is it," said Astrid. The woman in the picture was Alice Hickenhorn, and this was a representation of the moments before her death. Or, if myth were to be believed, moments before she was spirited away by fiery demons. "I've seen this picture elsewhere."

"We took a photo of this in the museum."

"The museum! Of course!"

Astrid compared the image and the patch of wool in her hands. The bearded man in the top corner was indeed wearing a tunic or some such, with a similarly distinctive pattern.

"What does it mean?" said Maddie.

"It means we should check it out," said Astrid. "To the museum!"

"You don't often hear people say that with that kind of enthusiasm," Maddie commented to Gregory.

"To the museum, I said!" Astrid commanded, pushing through the orchard back to the gap in the hedge.

14

Astrid began to unconsciously adopt a creepy, sidling gait as they approached the entrance to Wirkswell Museum.

"We don't have to sneak about," Maddie said. "It's a museum, and a free one at that."

"I have a complicated relationship with the management," said Astrid.

"What?"

"Never mind."

They went up the short flight of weathered steps and entered the museum. It was a modest-sized one, spread over three floors. In another life, Astrid had brought countless school trips here, gaggles of dead-eyed students with clipboards and worksheets and zero interest in Wirkswell's wool farming heritage, the development of a Georgian town, or even the one Joseph Wright painting the museum were lucky enough to own.

"You brought us here in year eight," said Maddie.

"Ah, you remember."

"I remember I got an over-priced pencil sharpener from the gift shop."

"And they say the British education system is the best in the world. This way."

They crept past a miniature model of the town and surrounding hills and moved through the historically nonsensical Mercian display and toward the sixteen hundreds.

There was a small selection of items relating to Burnbeck Mill and the businessman Samuel Atkins who had founded it. Astrid's eye was particularly drawn to blackened and misshapen thing which the museum had identified as *A grotesque pendant, perhaps made to ward off evil spirits.*

"There," said Astrid and pointed.

In one corner there was a display on the trial and attempted execution of Alice Hickenhorn. There were few genuine artefacts from the period, except for a spoon and rusted knife, and the pathetic fragments of a shoe, placed in a glass case in front of a display board. The board featured a blow-up of the same woodcut that Maddie's band had used for their album cover. There was Alice, tied to the stake, and the locals with flaming torches and, in the corner, was the belt-buckle hatted guy with the patterned tunic.

"You saying that wool was that item?" said Maddie.

"Don't be ridiculous," said Astrid. "No woollen garment is going to survive four hundred years in a compost here."

She read the text arranged around the image. Much of it was spurious and vague speculation and tenuous links to what was known. It included sections like *This man would have eaten a form of porridge for most meals and used a hand-carved spoon (see display case).* Next to the belt-buckle hatted guy was a paragraph that read *These fine gentlemen were possibly the Aldermen of the town and one of them might have been the mayor at the time, Roger Burnleigh. Note their fine shoes (see display case).*

"The mayor..." Astrid said. "It would be good to see the original tunic."

"Is this helping solve our time travel mystery?" said Maddie, sounding entirely like the bored school child on an unappreciated school trip.

"I wonder if the pattern is significant," Astrid mused.

"Astrid Bohart! You are barred and you know it!" shouted a woman, striding rapidly towards them.

"I'm just looking, Irma," Astrid snapped back.

The little museum clerk was putting far more arm motion into her striding than was really necessary, like she needed to somehow fill the space her body didn't naturally occupy.

"How can you be barred from a museum?" asked Maddie.

"Oh, ho, wouldn't you like to know!" said Irma with an evilly amused waggle of her eyebrows.

"If you stopped putting up historically dubious displays, I will stop correcting them," said Astrid.

"Correcting them? With spray paint? You're a vandal and a loony, Astrid, and you need medical help," said Irma.

"Woo, let's not be calling anyone loony," said Maddie.

"I'll call the police," said Irma.

"Because you're criminally misleading the public?" said

Astrid. "It's obvious to anyone with half a brain that the seventh to the ninth centuries never happened."

Maddie looked at her. "What?"

"Six fourteen to nine hundred and eleven to be precise," said Astrid.

Maddie's brow furrowed. "That's ... that's loony."

"Ha!" crowed Irma triumphantly.

"Uncover your eyes, you sheep!" Astrid shouted, addressing a wider audience that wasn't actually there.

"I'm beginning to wish we'd never come here," said Maddie.

Irma made to grab Astrid's hand, but Astrid was too quick and pulled it out of the way. However, her quick actions did not take into account how close Maddie was standing, and she slapped the back of her hand against Maddie's cheek.

Astrid's ears popped and everything went dark.

"Well, this is just brilliant," said Maddie in the darkness.

15

It took Astrid's eyes some time to adjust to the darkness. They were inside a room somewhere. That much was obvious. The air was filled with the smell of human habitation, of dust, of wood sap, of farting, sweating human bodies.

"Why did you do that?" Astrid hissed.

"Do what?" Maddie whispered in the dark.

"Zapped us away in time?"

"I did no such thing!"

"You're the one with the magic time-travelling friendship bracelet."

"Do you hear how stupid that sentence sounds? And why did you hit me?"

"Purely accidental."

"And you didn't think to tell me you were in trouble with the museum cops?"

Astrid tutted at her silliness. Then from outside there came a loud, self-important male voice.

"Bring her forth!"

There was a flickering light by which they could make out the edge of a doorway. Together, stumbling over the uneven floor, they crept over. The door was roughly made from wood: a thick shed door or something like it. It was not locked. Maddie pulled it open slightly.

Through the crack they could see out into the street.

It was Wirkswell, but it was clearly not the Wirkswell they knew. Astrid recognised the building across the way as the Swan Inn but it was the only recognisable building in sight. The timber-framed Tudor buildings would be long gone before their own time. The lacy collars and tall hats of the men with torches in the street only confirmed her worst suspicions.

"How far back did you bring us?" Astrid whispered.

Maddie squinted into the night. "I dunno. I'm not the history teacher. Oh, wait. This isn't—?"

Astrid didn't understand the sudden concern in Maddie's voice until she saw the timber stake in the centre of the street with piles of kindling banked around it.

"Sixteen oh-seven," she said.

There was a shout and then a ragged cheer from the men as a woman was dragged out of the Swan Inn. Her simple dress was ripped, her long hair wild and tangled about a dirty face.

"Think upon your actions, Master Burnleigh, please!" she shouted. Her voice carried but the tone of fear was unmistakeable. Astrid watched, fascinated.

"Poor girl," said Maddie.

"Yes, very sad," agreed Astrid because it seemed the appropriate thing to say. "Look, there. That must be the alderman fellow. Look at his tunic."

Maddie looked where directed. In the orange firelight, the bearded man's woollen robe was evident, as was the pattern of crosses on it.

"Same as the one in the compost," said Astrid.

"Bugger that," said Maddie. "What are we going to do?"

"Do you know how to make your bracelet do what it's told?"

"About Alice!" said Maddie passionately. "We are not going to just sit here and watch her burn."

"Thou art a depraved and wicked girl, Alice Hickenhorn!" a man shouted.

Astrid thought it hard to gauge Alice's age under all that muck, but she couldn't have been much more than her early twenties. Her fate was a matter of historical record.

"She doesn't die here," Astrid said.

Out in the street, a man shouted, "Commemorative sticks!" for some reason, and a local gave Alice an enthusiastic punch to the guts and helped drag her towards the stake.

"You sure about that?" said Maddie.

"It's part of the legend. As they attempt to burn her, fiery demons appear and spirit her away to hell or whatever."

"Uh-huh? And you think that's going to happen?"

"It's the historical account."

"So, we sit here and wait for actual, literal demons to appear?"

"I'm just saying. Is it really wrong to want to see history in action?"

"Fuck you, crazy bitch," said Maddie. "How can you be so calm about this?"

"Would matters be improved if I panicked and swore like a navvy?"

Maddie shuffled irritably, as though it was Astrid herself who was dragging the poor filthy wretch to her death. Astrid glanced about. Beyond the two dozen locals in the street, she tried to catch sight of the demons that would allegedly appear.

"I'm not saying they're going to be actual demons..." she mused. "Maybe she's rescued by, I don't know, a troupe of actors in costume."

"Really?"

"Or the gypsy folk come and get her."

"Travellers," said Maddie automatically.

"This is the past. It's okay to say gypsy now."

"I'm going to stop you there. Laying down an automatic veto on 'historically acceptable' racism."

"What?"

"If we travel back to Wild West times, I don't want you going all Quentin Tarantino on me and dropping 'n' words like confetti."

"What are you blathering about, girl?"

"I'm gabbling because I'm scared." She pushed the door wider to look about. By the stake, Alice Hickenhorn was fighting back tears, something clutched tightly in her fist. "Shit," said Maddie. "Where are they?"

"Any minute now..." said Astrid.

"Fiery demons."

"Is what they say."

Maddie expelled a loud and weary sigh and looked at Astrid. Maybe it was the look in Maddie's eyes. Maybe it wasn't. But the truth hit Astrid at that moment.

"It's us, isn't it?" she said.

"It's us," said Maddie. "We're Alice's demons."

"Fiery demons? We're just women."

Maddie glanced at the backpack on Astrid's back. "You still got some fireworks in there?"

Astrid knew she did. She pulled open the pack. She had half a dozen sparklers and a rocket.

"Right," said Maddie. "We go out, all sparkled up, yelling and screaming."

"And then what?"

"We grab Alice and ... take her to the next town over."

"Backnell?"

"Wherever. We stick her on a train."

"When do you think trains were invented?"

"Do not turn this into a history lesson. I'm miserable enough as it is."

There was no further time for discussion. Alice was going to die. Astrid put a sparkler in each of Maddie's hands then lit them, followed by two for herself.

"Let's go!" said Maddie and pushed her way out.

Maddie charged at the people, screaming in animal rage. Astrid followed swiftly after but decided to give her demon self a more measured personality. She bellowed deep and loud.

"I am the god of hellfire!" she began and then realised

she was going to sing *Fire* by – who was it? – Crazy Arthur Brown? Whichever, it was words and she yelled them as Maddie ran round in waggling lines, thrusting her sparklers at people.

The people of Stuart-era Wirkswell looked suitably stunned. Men fell back, the night lending extra depth to their alarm. Up on the pyre, Alice looked as equally shocked, although perhaps not afraid in quite the same way.

It was heartening to hear some of the folk mutter "Demons!" in shocked whispers.

"Give 'em the rocket!" Maddie snarled.

Astrid didn't need asking twice. She whipped the rocket out of her rucksack and, holding it by the wooden stick, dipped its taper in her sparkler flame.

"Fire!" she yelled. "To destroy all you've done!"

She waited for the rocket to ignite, to feel the first wash of fire up her arm before she let it go in the direction of the poshest men in the tallest hats. It struck ground and bounced. The men scattered.

Maddie had Alice by the hand and was pulling her away. By the time the rocket exploded (accompanied by many unmanly screams of terror) the three of them were running away. Maddie cast aside her sparklers and Astrid did likewise. They ran through the darkness, away from the lights of the town, up the hill.

16

Alice was saying something, over and over, but Astrid couldn't hear it on account of her own panting breath and creaking knees and the blood pumping in her ears. It was hard to see where they were going in the dark, but uphill seemed good. Uphill, away from the town in this direction, would lead them past the place where, in about four hundred years' time, Wirkswell Secondary High would stand, and on to the next town over.

Eventually Maddie, wheezing out of breath, waved her hands and they stopped.

Astrid looked back. There was no sign of pursuit from the town. The only light came from the moon and the stars. It was odd to be in a place where there was no light pollution at all, near or far.

"Think we lost them," she said.

"Are we stopping already?" said Alice.

"Give us a minute, Alice," said Maddie. "Jeez..."

"And then you take me to Satan's halls of Hell?"

Astrid scoffed at her. Then, struck by the ridiculousness of it all, laughed out loud. "Do we look like demons?"

Alice sniffed and wiped her nose. Her mucky face was wiped clean where the trail of snot went. She was a filthy creature. If Astrid was being charitable, she would say Alice looked like she'd been dragged through a hedge backwards. In truth, Alice's hair looked like the hedge itself, a mass of tangled cots and knots.

"You look like high born ladies," she declared. "I like your dress skirt," she said to Maddie.

"Thank you!" said Maddie. "Actually, it's a kilt."

"What's a kilt?"

"That's a dog blanket," said Astrid.

"You give blankets to dogs?"

"Actually, it's a Brownie blanket. Look. There's badges."

"Brownies?" said Alice, warily. "Pixies made it for you?"

"No. Not that kind of Brownie. I'm talking about the little people."

"So am I."

Astrid could see Alice start to shake. The enormity of what had happened was perhaps starting to hit her.

"Lend me your lighter," Maddie said.

Astrid passed it over and a flame flickered. Astrid heard a sucking sound.

"Are you lighting up?"

"For her nerves."

Maddie passed a roll up to Alice. "Suck on that, careful now."

"What is it?"

"Good for your nerves."

Cautiously, Alice reached for it and then drew on the joint. She did not cough as Maddie had perhaps expected, but simply froze in surprise, eyes wide.

"Did smoking exist in olden times?" said Maddie.

Astrid was about to answer (giving extra information on what the current king, James I, thought about tobacco), when she saw what it was that Alice held so tightly in her fist. A poorly carved head poked out from her encircling fingers. It was a carved wooden head Astrid knew perfectly well.

"Where did you get that?" Astrid demanded.

"What?" said Alice releasing a cloud of smoke.

"Where did you get that?!" Astrid spat.

"This? It's just my Polly Ann."

It was the same wooden doll that Astrid currently carried in her rucksack, the same one left to taunt her when the powers that be stole her teaching career and her credibility from her. Here it was again, a sure sign. Oh! She was fool! This had all seemed so convincing. The idiot woman, Maddie, and her ridiculous magic bracelet and then this extravagant charade.

"Oh, you had me convinced!" she said. She whirled around, wondering where the cameras were.

"About what?" said Maddie.

"Who paid you to do this, eh?"

"Huh?" There was brainless confusion on Maddie's face but Astrid saw through her now.

Astrid grabbed Alice's hand and the poppet doll it held. "This! This! It's not coincidence!"

"What are you doing?" said Alice, alarmed, and pulled back.

"Give it to me!"

Astrid tried to prise Alice's fingers apart. Alice (or the actress paid to play her!) started to struggle.

"Hey!" said Maddie and tried to physically intervene.

"You can't fool me! You can't fool me!" Astrid shouted for the benefit of whoever was watching. "I've seen this before!"

There was a change of light, a change of temperature, and Astrid felt herself drop several inches onto a hard wooden floor. The three women fell apart from one another. Maddie stumbled against a wooden table before landing on her backside.

They had jumped again. If this was special effects then Astrid had to concede the effects or the VR or the quality of the drugs she'd been given were something special.

Alice, who had dropped both joint and dolly in the time jumping transition, had fallen against a wall and now leaned on it to stay upright. She looked around the bright clean space, the sea of desks, the windows overlooking the playground, the overhead projector which was casting a PowerPoint onto the screen, and a little animated title screen which read, *What do we know about the Romans?*

"Am I in Heaven?" she whispered.

"No," whispered Astrid, recognising the room instantly.

"This is the green room of the Old Schoolhouse," said Maddie.

"It's my classroom," said Astrid.

Maddie picked up the smouldering roll-up and the dolly, and put them safely on the nearest desk. Alice approached the whiteboard and stretched her fingers into the beams of light that played on the board.

"It's beautiful," she whispered.

"I always did pride myself on the quality of my PowerPoints," said Astrid, then frowned. "When is this?"

Maddie shook her head. "Did you jump us here? Did I?" She went to the classroom door, peered through the glass and tried the door handle. "It's locked."

Astrid looked at the clock on the wall. "It's break time."

Alice ran her fingers over the animated Roman centurion. "Is this man trapped in a seeing glass?"

"It's a year seven topic," said Astrid. "Autumn term." She frowned and looked around the classroom for signs of when exactly this might have been.

"Someone's coming!" said Maddie. "We have to go."

"We don't know how we go?"

"Power of thought, I reckon," said Maddie. "Thoughts at the front of our minds. Alice, come here. I think we have to be in contact."

Maddie grabbed Alice's hand.

"Where are we going now?" asked Alice, excited rather than afraid.

"Wait," said Astrid. "I'm trying to work out where I am. When, I mean."

And then her eyes latched onto the joint and the dolly, sitting on her desk, the faintest wisps of smoke still curling above them.

"I think we should probably just discuss it in private," said a shadow at the door. Astrid recognised the voice of

Andrew Epping, the headteacher, her old boss, and she knew exactly where and when they were.

"No! Wait!" she said. "This is it! This is the moment!"

She pushed forward towards the desk, to grab the marijuana joint that would be her undoing, that *had* been her undoing. Andrew Epping would come in and see it and ask questions to which Astrid had no answers.

"Wait!" she grunted, but Maddie had hold of her.

"We have to go home!"

The light darkened a shade. There was suddenly noise all round them.

"Holy fuck!" yelled someone.

Alice stepped back and loudly put her foot through a bass drum laid on its side on the floor.

They were in the same room, but it was no longer the same room. The classroom had been cleared of desk and now the seats round the walls were filled with youths, the scruffiest kinds of youths, several with guitars or drumsticks in their hands. The closest were staring in shock at the women who'd just appeared in the room.

Astrid saw Maddie, coat in hand, running out of a far door and was about to shout after her when she realised Maddie was still next to her.

"Was that—?"

Maddie stared hollowly. "That was me. Running to the toilet to go time-travelling. For the first time."

"Where the hell did you come from?" a young man in need of a haircut demanded.

"Wirkswell," said Alice. "I'm having the most interesting day."

17

The three of them sat at a table in the bar of the Old Schoolhouse. Maddie had bought a pint of beer for herself and another for Alice. Astrid had wanted a gin and tonic, which cost twice as much as the two beers combined. For a time, the three of them just stared at their drinks before Alice said, “So, this is over four hundred years after my own time?”

“That’s right,” said Maddie, nodding sombrely.

“But I’m not all maggots and dust.”

“Seemingly not.”

Alice mused on that and sipped her beer. Her wild thatch of long hair didn’t look wholly out of place here. It had a sort of eighties back-combed goth vibe to it, although her filthy smock dress didn’t exactly sell the same image.

“So, it wasn’t MI5 or the World Bank who planted that marijuana on my desk,” said Astrid.

"It was never going to be MI5 or the World Bank," said Maddie. "Of all the theories—"

"So my article about the Phantom Time Hypothesis..."

"No one cared. No one cares," said Maddie and then patted her ex-teacher's hand. "Sorry."

"And does everyone in this age have the power to walk through time?" said Alice.

"I wouldn't call it power." Maddie lifted her hand to reveal her wrist and the friendship bracelet around it. "We don't understand it at all. If we're to get you back to your own time..."

"Do I have to go back to my own time?" said Alice.

Astrid and Maddie looked at one another. The questions piled up between them.

"Don't you want to go back to your own time?" said Astrid.

Alice scoffed. "Not likely, madam. You saw how shoddily treated I was. Nothing I want from there except—" She gasped and patted the wide pocket in the front of her dress. "Polly Ann!"

"We left it on Astrid's desk," said Maddie. "Sorry."

Astrid unzipped her rucksack, delved inside and pulled out the wooden dolly she'd been carrying all day. She placed it in front of Alice who snatched it up gleefully.

"Important to you?" said Maddie.

"My best friend, save the bees and my cow," said Alice.

"That's so sad," said Maddie.

"Tragic," Astrid agreed and raised her glass. "I suppose you can stay at mine. On the sofa, mind."

"So-fa," said Alice, trying the word.

"I have a spare bedroom, although I am putting you in a shower first."

"Shower?" said Alice.

"You smell. So bad."

"I smell as I always do," said Alice.

"It's an assault on the senses," said Astrid.

"Be nice," said Maddie.

"And then tomorrow we can work out how this time travel thing works."

Maddie shook her head. "The loop is broken. The next day is about to begin properly. We don't need to do anything."

"Forsake this power and go back to a humdrum life?" said Astrid with haughty humour. "Heavens, no. We plan our next jaunt."

"I don't think I need to go anywhere," said Maddie.

"You wouldn't want to time travel anywhere?"

"Anywhen," said Alice and seemed very pleased with herself.

"Where would I want to go?"

"When," said Alice, still very much pleased with herself.

"Turns out that there was a lorry coming the other way," said a man in leathers walking up to the bar with a mate. "He went straight across the white line and under the front wheels."

Maddie stood. "Excuse me."

The singer from the first band of the night turned and looked at her. "Oh, it's you."

"You're talking about Skid, right?"

"A dear friend."

"Yeah. Sorry about earlier. Um, when did he die?"

"Last Wednesday."

"Like the most recent Wednesday or...?"

"The Wednesday of last week."

"Right, right," said Maddie. "And the road he died on?"

"Why?"

"Please."

"The Baslow Road. Up by the Shell garage."

"Ah. I know the spot."

The guy shrugged at her. "Is that ... is that it?"

"Yeah, thanks. Very helpful."

He muttered something and moved on. Maddie turned to Astrid and Alice and gave them a cheerful, meaningful look that both of them failed to grasp.

"You want to time travel," she said.

Astrid sneered. "Go back and save the life of a man with the sobriquet Skid?"

"It's a start."

"Tell me more about this shower thing," said Alice.

ABOUT THE AUTHORS

Heide Goody lives in North Warwickshire with her family and pets.

Iain Grant lives in South Birmingham with his family and pets.

They are both married but not to each other.

ALSO BY HEIDE GOODY AND IAIN GRANT

Georgian Pineapple Shuffle

Leap into the time-bending adventure series that brings history to life with humour, adventure and heart.

Aspiring rock guitarist Maddie Waites, disgraced History teacher Astrid Bohart, suspected witch Alice Hickenhorn.

Three woman who discover the awesome ability to jump through time, decide to use that power to turn a quick profit and then make a complete mess of it.

It turns out that travelling back to Georgian times to sell exotic fruit to the aristocracy isn't as simple as one might think.

Prepare for double-crossing butlers, devious urchins and plundering the museum for dress-up fun.

These raucous and twisty novellas are perfect for fans of Jodi Taylor

Georgian Pineapple Shuffle

Clovenhoof

Getting fired can ruin a day...

...especially when you were the Prince of Hell.

Will Satan survive in English suburbia?

Corporate life can be a soul draining experience, especially when the industry is Hell, and you're Lucifer. It isn't all torture and brimstone, though, for the Prince of Darkness, he's got an unhappy Board of Directors.

The numbers look bad.

They want him out.

Then came the corporate coup.

Banished to mortal earth as Jeremy Clovenhoof, Lucifer is going through a mid-immortality crisis of biblical proportion. Maybe if he just tries to blend in, it won't be so bad.

He's wrong.

If it isn't the murder, cannibalism, and armed robbery of everyday life in Birmingham, it's the fact that his heavy metal band isn't getting the respect it deserves, that's dampening his mood.

And the archangel Michael constantly snooping on him, doesn't help.

If you enjoy clever writing, then you'll adore this satirical tour de force, because a good laugh can make you have sympathy for the devil.

Get it now.

Clovenhoof

Oddjobs

Unstoppable horrors from beyond are poised to invade and literally create Hell on Earth.

It's the end of the world as we know it, but someone still needs to do the paperwork.

Morag Murray works for the secret government organisation responsible for making sure the apocalypse goes as smoothly and as quietly as possible.

Trouble is, Morag's got a temper problem and, after angering the wrong alien god, she's been sent to another city where she won't cause so much trouble.

But Morag's got her work cut out for her. She has to deal with a man-eating starfish, solve a supernatural murder and, if she's got time, prevent her own inevitable death.

If you like The Laundry Files, The Chronicles of St Mary's or Men in Black, you'll love the Oddjobs series."If Jodi Taylor wrote a Laundry Files novel set it in Birmingham... A hilarious dose of bleak existential despair. With added tentacles! And bureaucracy!" – Charles Stross, author of The Laundry Files series.Oddjobs

Printed in Great Britain
by Amazon